I0529478

Lynton Viñas and Beowulf Perez:

Demon Slayers in the Taal Inferno

Graphic Depictions of the Battle

For a Soul

by

J. Wayne Frye

Illustrations and Photography

by

Lynd Ward

Freddie Perez

J. Wayne Frye

T.J.S. Conversion

Though the past Lynton adventures have been oriented toward the youth market, teachers should be aware that this edition is only suitable for older adolescents and adults. So please consider this as a strong cautionary advisory in relation to provocative/semi-nude illustrations and photographs as well as some mildly foul language.

Lynton Viñas and Beowulf Perez:
Demon Slayers in the Taal Inferno

The Author with the Real Lynton Viñas – Demon Fighter

About the Author

Wayne Frye's *Aaron Adams, Girl* series books and *Lynton* adventures are popular among mystery readers. He writes satirical political commentary for newspapers and his books on politics have created a great deal of controversy. He has written marketing/advertising textbooks, been a highly successful U.S. university hockey coach, professor, university president and served as a marketing consultant to hockey teams and motion picture companies. He has been cited for his work with inner-city gang children in the Los Angeles area and been active in the anti-globalization movement. He became a Canadian citizen in 2003 and lives in Ladysmith, British Columbia and Cavite, Philippines.

Other Books by J. Wayne Frye
Hockey Mania and the Mystery of Nancy Running Elk
Something Evil in the Darkness at Hopkins House
How Hockey Saved a Jew From the Holocaust:
The Rudi Ball Story
The Girl Who Stirred up the Whirlwind
The Girl Who Motivated Murder Most Foul
The Girl Who Said Goodbye for the Last Time
Fall From Apocalypse
Armageddon Now
Worth
When Jesus Came to Jersey as the Son of Thunder
When Jesus Came to Canada to Lead an Indigenous Rebellion
Canadian Angels of Mercy – Nurses in Times of Peril
Points of Rebellion: Aboriginals Who Fought for Justice
Lynton Curls Her Hair
Lynton Buys a New Cell-Phone
and Hears the Voice of Doom
Lynton Walks on Water
Lynton and the Vampire at Tagaytay Manor
Chablis: Avenging Angel for the Forgotten
In the City of Lost Hope
Chablis and the Terrorist Who Resurrected the Spirit of Che
Pursuit
Sammy Sasquatch and the Sts'ailes Star
The Mouse That Saw Everything in Black and White

J. Wayne Frye

Lynton Viñas and Beowulf Perez: Demon Slayers in the Taal Inferno

TABLE OF CONTENTS

Introduction - 5

Excite, Titillate and Motivate

Prologue - 9

Not Easy This Time

Chapter 1 - 17

We Must Not Tarry

Chapter 2 - 39

The Demon Slayer was on the Job

Chapter 3 - 59

Mighty Warrior into the Lion's Den

Chapter 4 - 93

Go and Meet Your Fate

Chapter 5 - 123

The Full-Moon on Their Side

Chapter 6 - 159

Out Into the Sunshine of Hope

Where Peace and Tranquility Reigned

Epilogue - 175

His Life Slowly Ebbed Away

Lynton Viñas and Beowulf Perez:
Demon Slayers in the Taal Inferno

To: **Hannah** – like Lynton, dedicated to fair play and justice and to **Robert**, Lynton's brother who knows the value of a sister filled with love and compassion.

Catalogue Number: 8341-945-849

ISBN: 978-1-928183-16-7

Fireside Books – Victoria, British Columbia

Is an Imprint of

Peninsula Publishing Consortium

Lynton Viñas and Beowulf Perez: Demon Slayers in the Taal Inferno

INTRODUCTION
EXCITE, TITILLATE AND MOTIVATE

The Mighty Taal Volcano and Taal Island where this adventure occurred.

O.K., here we go with the first pictorial book about the gosh-darnest, most incredible demon fighter to ever come out of the Philippines. Her exploits have been recorded in detail in the books: *Lynton Curls Her Hair, Lynton Buys a New Cell-Phone and Hears the Voice of Doom, Lynton Walks on Water and Lynton and the Vampire at Taygaytay Manor.* Why did I decide to do a picture/illustrations book? Simply because the adult readers of the aforementioned books have asked to see more of Lynton's physical appearance. The small number of illustrations in previous books that also included her loyal companions Channa and Ingrid have garnered rave reviews and stimulated interest from people wanting to see more of her physical attributes that certainly match up to her highly honed demon fighting skills.

I am one who likes to keep my books packed with action and always hopefully generate genuine heartfelt sympathies for the downtrodden who toil for their daily bread in relative obscurity. There are many types of demons, and the cruellest demons on the planet are real live people and corporations that neglect the human equation in everything they do and allow greed to control their actions. This is an abomination to the concept of true fairness and justice that is so gloriously and freely ballyhooed in democracies all across the world that use elections every few years to allow the people to vote, not on genuine leaders, but rather on who will be their oppressors for the next few years. The demon of greed and self-interest is the fiercest demon of all.

Lynton Viñas and Beowulf Perez:
Demon Slayers in the Taal Inferno

Here fans is a book about one of Lynton's most thrilling adventures illustrated with photos and dramatic drawings along with computer generated depictions of an extraordinary woman who brings meaning to the phrase "Demon Fighter." We all fight our individual and mass demons each and every day. A world that aggrandizes greed as an enviable trait and lavishly rewards those at the top of the economic ladder while unceremoniously relegating the rest of us to little more than economic slavery is actually filled with the most abominable demons imaginable who are driven by their insatiable desire to acquire more and more with no regard for whom they crush along the way.

This was certainly not a very easy book to write, because the subject is truly a captivatingly remarkable woman with absolutely incredible attributes of compassion for the downtrodden of the world who are always, by virtue of dire circumstances, on the outside looking in with little hope of ever rising above their lot in life. Her sense of fair play and justice, dedication to those in pain and stubborn refusal to accept things as they are rather than strive to make them as they should be, makes writing about her more joy than work.

Now, when it comes to illustrating a book, which I have never done before, this was actually a monumentally taxing endeavour, as proper lighting, contrasting and posing was often almost impossible to achieve. Thanks to the assistance of Lynd Ward, Freddie Perez, Henry Fuseli and T.J.S. Conversion, the task was fairly well-accomplished in often very difficult circumstances.

This is a Lynton adventure like no other and is also a little more adult oriented than the normal. The artists here have captured her with great skill as they have seen her pictures and real-life magnificence that allowed them to effectively interpret her beauty of heart, body and soul. So, sit back in your favourite easy chair and let's begin a journey with Lynton that will hopefully excite, titillate, motivate and never make you eviscerate.

Lynton Viñas and Beowulf Perez:
Demon Slayers in the Taal Inferno

PROLOGUE
NOT EASY THIS TIME

Beowulf Perez was a born in Samar Province in the Philippines. How he came to Manila no one knew. Maybe even he did not know. He was probably around 30 years old, but he was not sure, because there was no formal record of his birth. His mother gave birth to him in a field near an old farmhouse and after the birth she just left him lying there, assuming some wild animal would make him its prey, and her unwanted child would never be a burden on her. Well, he was never a burden on her, but that wild prey did not devour him, rather he was found by a kindly old lady who always wanted children but had never been able to have any. Having once read the epic poem Beowulf about a brave fighter for justice, she called him by that name, which was usually shortened to Beo by those who knew him. He began life as an orphan and had to struggle to survive in a very hostile environment, except for the kind old woman.

Unfortunately, the old woman's husband was not so kind and always looked upon Beowulf as a slave rather than a son. The woman tried desperately to control her husband's violent outbursts with Beowulf, but was unable to do so. When he was 12, he told his mom that he could no longer tolerate the abuse and left home.

No one knew when Beowulf seemed to acquire mystical powers, but once when he was selling kitchen towels as a street peddler, a priest was relating to a vendor how a young girl was seemingly possessed by a demon, he casually asked the priest if he really believed in demons. The priest replied, "I certainly do young man, and so should you. Demons are among us."

Beowulf said, "Yes, they are among us, but they are not the supernatural kind of demons. Go to the halls of government where politicians abuse the people's trust and there you will find demons of neglect. Go to the corporations that have no heart and no compassion and there you will find demons of greed. Go to the streets here in Manila where people have to fight to survive each day and you will find the demons of cruelty. Go to the courts of this land where the poor are unceremoniously carted off to jail and you will see that only the wealthy receive justice. Go to your church that preaches children must be born, but does nothing to assure those children have shelter, food and healthcare. Demons are among us yes, but demons made by man."

Impressed with the young man's intensity and perceptiveness, the priest took him to the church, where he became a trusted servant in the home for priests. There, he learned the Bible for the first time and the priests all saw in him the heart of an angel but the determined will of a warrior. Beowulf grew into a man of character who stood against the tyranny of poverty, neglect and indifference. When the church turned its back on injustice, it was Beowulf who would boldly go forth and fight battles the church was too timid to fight. He became a bulwark of trust and devotion to the causes of those who needed a lift up, and in the process he was unflinching in his demands for justice and fair-play to the point he would often resort to threats of violence, and his towering bulk, bulging muscles and demeanour would often strike fear into the hearts of miscreants.

Lynton Viñas and Beowulf Perez:
Demon Slayers in the Taal Inferno

The physical contrasts between Beowulf and the famous demon fighter in Cavite, Lynton Viñas, were fairly well-pronounced, whereas Beowulf stood 6:0, Lynton was a demure 5:2. Beowulf weighed 90 kilos with his sinewy body glistening with power. On the other hand, Lynton weighed a mere 53 kilos with the most muscular part of her body being the calves of her legs which had been developed through many years as a volleyball player and dancer. Because of playing volleyball, like Beowulf, Lynton had strong upper body strength, as attested to by a former boyfriend she caught with another woman. He also found out she had a vicious left hook that could fell an opponent with one mighty blow.

The physical differences were visible to the naked eye, but hidden from the eye was the intensity of the mind Lynton possessed. Like Beowulf, she was fearless when confronted by those who dared perpetrate physical violence upon the weak. And when it came to combating the mental cruelties displayed by those who preyed upon the unsuspecting and misfortunate, neither one of them would yield before hopelessness.

Lynton Viñas and Beowulf Perez:
Demon Slayers in the Taal Inferno

This is obviously a story devoted to Lynton Viñas, but like previous adventures that included her friends Channa and Ingrid, this tale of a mighty mission to take on demons cannot be told without including another one of her friends this time, Beowulf Perez, for he, too, is a renowned demon fighter, and it is he who decided that when assigned a task by the church that had to be kept secret, he knew there was only one woman in all of the Philippines capable of taking on the task that would require a herculean effort to save a girl from doom.

So, once again she journeys to Tagaytay where two of her previous adventures took place. This time, she will go to a small village at the base of a volcano where a young woman has been possessed by one of history's most fearsome demons, and time is of the essence, because the previous 47 possessions all occurred in a four month time line and only a few days remained for the demon fighter to rescue this young woman from the clutches of an insidious demon.

There are many who sing the praises of Lynton, but few ever really realized just how many times she has come up against evil, looked it in the eye and come out triumphant. It would not be easy this time.

Beowulf Perez at 19 (Taken in Manila)

Lynton Viñas at 22 (Her demon fighting skills had not appeared at this time)

Lynton Viñas and Beowulf Perez:
Demon Slayers in the Taal Inferno

Lynton Appearing in an NBC Ad for the never aired show *Handbag Hell* on Times Square.

Lynton appearing on an ad for a Yankee Stadium concert with her friends (Channa and Ingrid)

Lynton Viñas and Beowulf Perez:
Demon Slayers in the Taal Inferno

Below: Lynton with her two demon fighting companions: Ingrid and Channa

Lynton Viñas and Beowulf Perez:
Demon Slayers in the Taal Inferno

CHAPTER 1
WE MUST NOT TARRY

Episode 1

Praise for the prowess of kings and queens of justice dance like stars on a cloudless night. This is not an oft told tale even in the Philippines, as it seems too fantastic for belief. Yet, all honour and praise is due Beowulf and Lynton who together squandered foes of decency from many a source. In poverty they both came up, and people far and near actually sensed a glow that flowed from them as if there was something divine about each. Neither one of them realized their mandate for demon fighting until later in life.

Lynton was an heir to nothing but poverty; however, it was if from heaven she was sent to favour folk, because she felt their woe. Her land had a benevolent dictator who was sometimes given to rage against his foes, but he fell from grace so the poor lost shelter and their rice, as he was replaced by those who bowed to corporate greed. So, in some cases the

Lynton Viñas and Beowulf Perez:
Demon Slayers in the Taal Inferno

poor can benefit more from a benevolent dictator than democracy, as in today's world, places like the USA use democracy as a code word for what amounts to the exploitation of the masses so the 1% at the top are able to enjoy lives of splendorous excess on the backs of cheap labour.

Though she barely knew the times in her homeland when there was more affluence, Lynton came into a world of want to be a wielder of wonder in the places of poverty. She became world renown as a defender of justice for the downtrodden. Before long she was tagged demon fighter because circumstances put her into Dante's Inferno, where she freed two souls from torture deep within the pits of hell.

Even as a child she was on her own, because she had parents who were more child-like than she was. On the streets at 12, men came calling to no avail, but she did accept those men she looked upon as warriors who wanted to fight for justice. Her lauded deeds brought honour to her gang that ruled the streets. They exacted justice for those who got none. Hers was a gang that had morals and sided with

Lynton Viñas and Beowulf Perez:
Demon Slayers in the Taal Inferno

those who had no one to give them a hand up in a society that rewarded those at the top at the expense of those at the bottom. Lynton was on the streets, because she wanted to give her mom and dad one less mouth to feed, and she struggled each day selling fruits and vegetables, usually spending the night in some alleyway. Valiantly, she battled her way out of abject poverty to reach the pinnacle of success as defined by a society where everyone is judged by the size of their bank account rather than the size of their character. Yet, her success was not based upon the accumulation of wealth, but upon the thousands of people who looked up to her and knew that in the woman called by her biographer *the dynamic dynamo* beat the heart of a champion among the people, a person who stood tall against the injustice of a world based on greed and indifference.

Beowulf, like Lynton, elicited respect and admiration from those who knew him. He was an astute man whom the church had slowly come to rely upon in times of peril. The priests had been approached about a young girl who had seemingly become possessed by the spirit of a demon. The Vatican would not approve an exorcism, so Father Mendez came to Beowulf and asked if he might do something without a sanction from the church. Thus began a friendship between Beowulf and Lynton, for that very day he hopped into a riggity smoke-belching antiquated old Jeepney and journeyed to the home of Lynton Viñas in the Old Bulihan area of Cavite.

Jeepney – chief mode of transport in Philippines.

Beowulf asked the Jeepney driver if he knew where he might find the home of Lynton Viñas. The driver looked over his shoulder with deep intensity as he said, "Lynton? Everybody knows her home. You getting ready to fight some demons?"

"Just looking to discuss a few very important things with her."

Lynton Viñas and Beowulf Perez: Demon Slayers in the Taal Inferno

With a look of deep reverence, the driver offered a cogent observation. "That girl is more saintly than Mother Teresa was, but let me tell you if you want an ass-kicking demon fighter ain't nobody better, and I am talking about supernatural demons and the real bad demons – the human kind. That girl 'ill take 'um all on. Yep, Lynton is a demon-fightin' dynamo."

Just as Beowulf was about to interrupt, the driver signalled no and continued. "She once took on the barangay captain in a boxing match for charity and she whipped his ass good. Had him down for the count in only one minute of round one. We all laughed our asses off as she bent over to help the poor guy up from the canvas, because he was so groggy he thought he had done been dispatched to the promised land. Mighty Filipino boxer, Manny Pacquiao, could a took out that barangay captain no sooner than she did. That left hook of hers is dynamite."

Meanwhile, the other riders all started nodding in vehement agreement with the driver. One of them said, "Yep, that girl can do some real damage with that left hook."

Lynton Viñas and Beowulf Perez:
Demon Slayers in the Taal Inferno

Another rider enthusiastically chimed in, "And them high heels of hers. Wow, oh my, oh my, they are deadly. Look out; she once put two bad guys down in Taygaytay into a permanent coma with those deadly instruments. They are four spiked inches of pure terror when she cocks up one of her muscular legs and delivers a blow between the legs. Wham, bam and thank you ma'am."

Everyone started laughing and an old woman offered her observation. "Told my husband when he started to hit me that if he laid one hand on me I was going to get Lynton Viñas and her heels from hell over to our house and his balls would be up in his throat before he had a chance to say he was sorry. Man is scared to death of me now, cause he knows Lynton is my friend. She's the friend of anybody who is down and out and getting pushed around. She'll take on the President of this here country if need be. She ain't afraid of nobody."

Thrilled with the reverence showed Lynton by all aboard the Jeepney, Beowulf said, "But I need to find where she lives."

Lynton Viñas and Beowulf Perez: Demon Slayers in the Taal Inferno

At that very moment, the Jeepney turned down an alleyway and 50 metres down the driver came to a halt with his badly worn brakes screeching a symphony of neglect. "For anyone wanting to see her, I make a special detour." He pointed to an almost new food stand built out of plastic and there was Lynton, holding a child and smiling. "There she be my friend. Damn, seems like she has a halo around her." People in the Jeepney nodded in agreement as Beowulf said thanks, bent down and waddled his way out of the Jeepney. He plopped onto the street and there she was shining like a beacon in the darkness.

Lynton Viñas and Beowulf Perez:
Demon Slayers in the Taal Inferno

Forth fared Beowulf at the fated moment, basking in the glow of an angel, but was she an angel of light, or an avenging angel, or maybe both? He approached her with reverence and as she turned toward him, her smile and twinkling eyes bespoke of someone with the soul of kindness and the heart of concern, but alongside those attributes was the countenance of a warrior.

Extending his hand he said, "I am Beowulf Perez and I come to you with an urgent request."

Lynton, seeing the consternation in his eyes, handed the child back to its mother and replied, "Come with me to my humble abode and tell me of your woe. I can see you are troubled."

Sharing a cup of coffee, Beowulf related that there were forces at work that were trying to destroy a young girl, and that the Pope would not approve an exorcism for a reason that was never explained. He wanted her to go with him to visit a group of priests who would lay out what was necessary to free this girl from torment."

Lynton Viñas and Beowulf Perez:
Demon Slayers in the Taal Inferno

Lynton scoffed at superstition, and often saw religion as a hindrance rather than a help in the elevation of humanity. Still, she knew that there were unexplainable forces at work in a world where the fiercest demons were the demons of poverty, injustice and indifference. She, herself, had faced those demons all her life, and in one of her most noted adventures she had descended into a form of hell to battle a demon called Belmoda. There she had reached a heart no one thought he had and watched a tear gently float down his cheek.

Beowulf looked at her almost pleading. He said, "She is a fine young woman with promise, and the priests want to help but must follow the edicts of the Vatican."

"The Vatican, the White House, Downing Street, the Kremlin; the seats of power are too far removed from the people for those who rule to understand how they cry for justice. If leaders lived the lives of those they lead there might be more sympathy. However, how can a person living in royal splendour understand the plight of the woman who lives in a hovel, walks a

Lynton Viñas and Beowulf Perez:
Demon Slayers in the Taal Inferno

kilometre to get water every day and watches her baby go to bed crying of hunger? The world is ruled by and for the 1% and the rest of us are rarely even afterthoughts in the grand scheme of things. Of course, I will help. Let us go and talk to those who are part of the problem and can't see that their own prejudices and judgements of others trap far too many in the pit of despair."

This young woman lived on a tiny island on a lake where the mighty Taal Volcano in Taygaytay jutted skyward and belched out its smoke as if within its fiery pits the demons of darkness were cavorting in a dance of despair and turmoil that would embrace mankind with an evil which was so insidious it would destroy the souls of anyone unlucky enough to incur the wrath of the ones who served Beelzebub – the tyrannous ruler of that dark underworld where the villainy of the vanquished lived to capture soul after soul in its grasp.

In Taal Lake near Taygaytay, Philippines lies a tiny village at the base of the mighty Taal Volcano. Lynton and Beowulf took a boat from Taygaytay to the village

26 **J. Wayne Frye**

Lynton Viñas and Beowulf Perez:
Demon Slayers in the Taal Inferno

of perhaps 200 people where Sarafina Sanchez, a young girl of 15 was battling against what had been determined by a local priest as a demon.

Lynton and Beowulf Took
the Below Boat to the Village

The people of the village greeted the two like conquering heroes, as they had all heard of Lynton and knew of her exploits as two of her most well-known adventures took place in nearby Taygaytay where she battled a vampire and also in nearby Taal Heritage Village where she took on a religious charlatan.

Lynton Viñas and Beowulf Perez:
Demon Slayers in the Taal Inferno

The two were placed on donkeys and were born forth to the centre of the little place by the adoring villagers, where they were met by the village headman, Alberto Orpiano, who had worrisome and winsome words for them. "Welcome my friends to our small village where we are all family, which is why the agony of Sarafina Sanchez is the agony of us all."

Lynton, who was sitting on a small wooden bench, leaned slightly forward and said, "What does the priest say?"

"Ah, we have sent for him. He is on the far side of the island visiting with a sick old woman, but he will make haste to return as he is anxious to talk with you."

Just then a beautiful young girl walked up and whispered in Alberto's ear. He looked up at her and smiled as he said, "Yes, this is them. Lynton and Beowulf, I want you to meet Sarafina Sanchez, a very smart, and, obviously, as you can see, beautiful young woman. We are very proud of her, as she has already been offered a scholarship to T.U.P."

J. Wayne Frye

Lynton Viñas and Beowulf Perez:
Demon Slayers in the Taal Inferno

Lynton got up and extended her hand, and Sarafina shyly shook it. Beowulf then stood, extended his hand and said, "My, you are indeed a beautiful young woman."

Lynton said, "You already have a scholarship at 15, and to Technological University of the Philippines. Let me guess – engineering, right?"

Smiling joyously, she replied, "Yes, but I shall be 16 in two weeks, and I am graduating high school early as I made two grades in one year. And yes, I want to study engineering."

Lynton Viñas and Beowulf Perez:
Demon Slayers in the Taal Inferno

Just then the priest walked up. "Good day Ms. Viñas and to you also Mr. Perez." He then turned very sternly to Sarafina and said, "Would you excuse us my dear?"

Sarafina meekly bowed her head and said "Goodbye."

After Sarafina demurely lowered her head and left, Lynton said, "Father, do you think it appropriate to dismiss her when we are about to talk about her problems?"

Very rigid in his bearing and a stern look upon his face, Father Vasquez very pointedly and sarcastically said, "I represent the church and I shall decide what is best for the child."

Lynton rose up from her seat, looked him directly in the eyes and said, "Well, maybe I should leave then. I was under the impression the church wanted me here." She then looked over at Beowulf and continued, "You can stay if you want. I am not going to be bullied by a man who thinks because he is a priest I am supposed to bow before him like he was some kind of royalty."

As she turned to leave, Alberto leapt up and said, "No, no, please Ms. Viñas, we need you. We know of your reputation and we do need you, and, of course, Mr. Perez, too."

Father Vasquez, somewhat contrite, but still with a tinge of arrogance, said, "Perhaps we got off on the wrong foot. If so, I think we can forget it and move forward for the sake of the child. She is in great danger."

Lynton, noticing that Father Vasquez pointedly avoided indicating he was sorry, said with determination, "Then it behoves us all to marshal our resources and put aside personal feelings. However, it should be clear that I respect the church, but I am a free and independent thinker and will not bow to you, sir, just because you are a priest. If I think you are wrong, I will tell you so, and you are perfectly welcome to do the same with me. Do we understand each other?"

Lynton Viñas and Beowulf Perez:
Demon Slayers in the Taal Inferno

Now, more contrite, and showing a sense of respect for this extraordinarily strong woman, Father Vasquez said, "Yes, we do, indeed."

Lynton, easing back into her chair and said, "So, tell us of what has been occurring."

Father Vasquez took a deep breath, sighed and began. "Well, about four months ago, Sarafina was guiding some tourists up to the volcano, and they got there when it was almost dark. The tourists heard a strange sound coming from the caldera of the volcano. They swore that suddenly up through the water and steam rose a dragon like creature, but only for a second or two and it looked at Sarafina and she collapsed. They placed her on a donkey and brought her back. She was in a comatose state for about a day, but before the doctor arrived, she came out of it. Oh, but how she came out of it. She was shouting obscenities. This from a girl whom no one had ever heard utter a profane word. Oh, and suddenly she began to look at the humble surroundings and told her parents that they should never have had seven children since they were so poor."

Lynton Viñas and Beowulf Perez:
Demon Slayers in the Taal Inferno

Lynton nodded her head knowingly and said to the father, "So far, the girl is making sense. Seems to me like she is pretty perceptive."

Father Vasquez, seemingly upset, replied, "The church has strict rules about birth control, and they are good Catholics."

"Good Catholics should worry about feeding their children, and having too many when you are poor makes that very difficult. However, we are not here to debate church doctrine, but to see if we can help Sarafina, so please continue. I am sorry I interrupted you."

"So, after that initial outburst, all seemed fine until about a week later. Sarafina woke the whole family up screaming one night and they rushed into the living room as she sometimes sleeps on the floor there. What they saw brought them horror as they had never known before. Sarafina was levitating, floating above the floor maybe four feet into the air. The father went to her, but some force threw him back against the wall. The entire family trembled in fear. Then Sarafina

Lynton Viñas and Beowulf Perez:
Demon Slayers in the Taal Inferno

again started shouting obscenities as she was floating about. She gradually floated to the floor where she was as stiff as a board and popped up erect and her eyes were glowing like fires in the pits of hell. She uttered in a deep vile male voice, I am Elashabab, dragon demon of the Caldera and I shall bring ruin upon this girl and this family. My evil rivals that of Belmoda, evil minion of despair. I shall devour her soul until it is mine, and I will eat the hearts of her family and regurgitate them into the pit of fire that burns below the caldera where I rise to bring ruin to all who do not bow in supplication before the devil who reigns supreme over the bowels of the earth."

Lynton said, "Are you 100% sure she said Belmoda?"

"Yes, Ms. Viñas. That is why we wanted you, because we know you are familiar with Belmoda and it has been rumoured that you battled him once before."

Lynton, ever sceptical, replied, "I am not sure what I battled in a dark pit one night, but I know the stories of

Lynton Viñas and Beowulf Perez:
Demon Slayers in the Taal Inferno

Belmoda and his evil. Real or imagined, this is very serious business. Please go on. What else happened?"

Father Vasquez continued. "After that night, I was called in and tried to counsel them as best I could. I even asked for an exorcism, but the Vatican denied the request. For what reason, I do not know, but they turn more requests down than they ever honour, so I was not too surprised. Nonetheless, the evil continued to manifest itself within Sarafina every three or four days, and each episode got worse. Once she spit out disgusting green slime upon her parents and siblings, calling them vile names and promising to wreck havoc upon them if they did not go from her sight as she found them disgusting to look upon. Her siblings have all been dispatched to aunts, uncles and grandmother in Taygaytay. The fear in that home where evil has manifested itself is so immense that you can almost cut it with a knife."

Beowulf jumped up, looked over at Lynton who nodded yes, as she knew what he was thinking. "Yes, we need to go to the house now."

Lynton Viñas and Beowulf Perez:
Demon Slayers in the Taal Inferno

Father Vasquez, realizing the necessity for haste, said, "Of course, but we must be careful that Sarafina is not made aware of how much trouble awaits her, because the demon is getting stronger. I can sense it."

Beowulf heatedly interjected, "The time is absolutely critical for Sarafina. There cannot be much of it left for the poor girl if the demon, as you indicate, is getting stronger. I have been at exorcisms and know from experience that once the demon has corrupted the mind so totally and indisputably the process of reversing the damage is almost impossible. I genuinely fear that Sarafina has reached that stage where great difficulties await us."

Father Vasquez sighed and said, "I, too, have been at exorcisms and I have seen the power of evil that oft times appears to trump the power of good. Evil is like a pernicious seed that grows and grows and produces a giant tree whose shade casts darkness over other trees that eventually wilt and die as they cannot get the sunlight needed to grow. Sarafina is being denied the light of good."

Lynton Viñas and Beowulf Perez: Demon Slayers in the Taal Inferno

Beowulf, with great sincerity in his voice, said, "We must find that tree that has sprouted within her, cull it from the forest so that she can get the sunlight she needs to survive."

"My dear friends," said a concerned Lynton, "we have a great task at hand, and it will demand great effort and sacrifice. I have seen the work of demons before, both the supernatural kind and the much worse kind – those that prey upon the unsuspecting in every day life. Both are sinister in intent, and both can suck the life out of the victims. This is not a task I take lightly, because I know the risks involved, and what we are about to face is a terror that most people run from in mortal fear. Are you both sure that you are up to the task?"

They both nodded their heads vehemently in the affirmative, and Beowulf smiled as he said, "You know it!"

Lynton looked Father Vasquez directly in the eyes and said, "Sarafina is marked with the sign of the devil. Look upon her and you will see a pentagram somewhere. If not on her, it is near where she sleeps. I have dealt with this before. Sometimes it is the individual who is simply trying to convince themselves that evil is overtaking them. However, time is of the essence. We must not tarry."

J. Wayne Frye's Altered Lynton Depiction
Title: *Demon Fighter's Arrow of Justice*

J. Wayne Frye

Lynton Viñas and Beowulf Perez:
Demon Slayers in the Taal Inferno

CHAPTER 2
THE DEMON SLAYER WAS ON THE JOB

Weapons of war and weeds of indignation
Flowed within her mind like mighty waves
Upon a tumultuous sea in a raging storm
Of disgust and moral rebuke.
With her friend Beowulf by her side
Lynton was ready to go into combat
Against evil that lurked in the darkness.

Watching Lynton was like observing hope in motion. She walked into Sarafina's home and her parents, Darlene and Richard, extended the hand of thanks, as you could see in their eyes the sense that the salvation of their daughter rested in the hands of the dynamic dynamo.

With a golden breastplate of determined hope rising and falling with each intake of air, Lynton's alluringly sensuous perky breasts for some reason caught Beowulf's eyes and he felt a slight sexual arousal as Lynton scanned the room like a cougar stalking its prey.

Lynton Viñas and Beowulf Perez:
Demon Slayers in the Taal Inferno

Sarafina walked in and you could see hope on her face as she greeted the three, but, for some reason, she held Lynton's hand longer, and there was something there that the others did not notice. There was an evil to the warmth of her hand, and Lynton, looking into her eyes, held the grip tighter and tighter until she finally said to Sarafina, "To whom do I speak. Who is it that wants the soul of this child?"

Suddenly, in a deep, coarse tone that seemed to arise from the dark, deep bowels of evil came a shattering voice that literally vibrated off the walls of Sarafina's home. Laughing as if delighted to face the greatest demon fighter of the all, the voice almost danced in evil merriment. "I am Belmoda's son, the one who rises from the depths of the crater of fire."

Lynton, without any hesitation or fear, very calmly said, "I have fought your father and won, his evil tempered with tears of sympathy. Be gone from this child. I know you, because you were by your father's side in the inferno in which my mind meandered to free two souls from a house of evil. Your name, tell me your name dragon of despair who belches fire from that volcano which leads into the hell of the mind. Mighty Taal is your home because of its roaring fires of fury, but this child's mind offers no respite."

The others stood in awe as the dynamic dynamo, in shorts and a tank top looked like a soldier in battle against a foe. Elevating herself on the Nike shoes given her when she was a background singer for an ad the company did, she purposefully made herself slightly taller than Sarafina so that she could look down into her eyes rather than stare straight ahead and let the entity sense equality with her power.

The sound of swirling wind could be heard and again the walls vibrated with evil intentions as the entity sternly said, "I am Elashabab, first son of Satan's strong right arm Belmoda. I am a proud Kenite of the first order, descended from the grand line of history's first murderer, Cain. I am of the serpent seed, the very seed that tempted Eve. My brother is Abbaddon, and together, we reside in the bowels of the Taal Volcano where we incubate and develop our power. I am the dragon of despair that devours souls and feasts at the table of humanity."

Lynton Viñas and Beowulf Perez:
Demon Slayers in the Taal Inferno

Elashabab was often drawn as a dragon during the Middle Ages and Sarafina saw him as a dragon when she went to the summit of the Taal Volcano.

Lynton looked over at Father Vasquez and said, "Bring your crucifix."

Tepidly, he handed it to her, but made sure to steer clear of Sarafina. Lynton held it up before Sarafina and said, "Do you fear this?"

Again, in the gruff, coarse male voice from Sarafina's mouth came these words: "You whore

Lynton Viñas and Beowulf Perez: Demon Slayers in the Taal Inferno

harlot I spit on the crucifix." Then, Sarafina's head swivelled to her left, and staring at the trembling Father Vasquez said, "And I defecate on the church and those who represent it."

A stillness came over the room as Sarfina raised her hand and pointed at Father Vasquez. "He trembles because he fears me more than he loves God. His God is disgusting and powerless against my beloved Satan."

Sarafina's parents and Father Vasquez were shivering with fear, but Lynton and Beowulf not once showed any trepidation in the face of evil. In fact, Lynton smiled in Sarafina's face and said, "I am coming for you Elashabab. I am walking into your lair and slaying you. My friend Beowulf and I eat dragons of despair for breakfast and regurgitate them into the slimy swamps that can swallow them into the muck and mire where they belong. I don't fear you. I fear no man, no God, nothing of this earth, heaven nor hell. I strip myself bare before you, because I am a woman with no shame." To the surprise of all there, Lynton began undressing, never taking her eyes off Sarafina.

Lynton Viñas and Beowulf Perez:
Demon Slayers in the Taal Inferno

Naked before all, she said, "I am Lynton Viñas, demon fighter and saver of souls that have been devoured by the detestable creatures from the pits of eternal fire. I am pure with no shame."

Beowulf then moved slightly behind Lynton and removed his clothes as he said, "I, too, have no shame. I bare myself before all with humility and vow to be by this woman's side when she slays you!"

Suddenly, a bright light seemed to shine down from above on Lynton and a lesser one on Beowulf, as Father Vasquez turned his head to avoid seeing the nakedness, or perhaps to avoid stimulation. Suddenly, the plant beside Lynton seemed to grow larger and larger and slimy water formed on the floor.

Lynton Viñas and Beowulf Perez:
Demon Slayers in the Taal Inferno

Then, Sarafina pointed down at the floor where an image of a skull materialized. "I will devour your flesh and leave nothing but bone, bitch."

The battle between Lynton and the demon had started in earnest now, and the demon within Sarafina

Lynton Viñas and Beowulf Perez:
Demon Slayers in the Taal Inferno

was trying to instil fear in a woman who had none. Slowly, the image of the skull grew larger and larger, which made Lynton feel smaller and smaller. It was intimidation, and Lynton, despite all that was happening still knew that it could all just be an illusion caused by hypnotic power used by Sarafina. She was acknowledging the demon, but knew all that was happening could simply be mass hypnotic suggestion caused by the mind of Sarafina. Still, as she talked, in her own mind the skull grew larger and larger until she felt miniscule before it.

Lynton Viñas and Beowulf Perez:
Demon Slayers in the Taal Inferno

Sarafina pointed at Beowulf and he collapsed onto the floor quivering for a few seconds until he lay perfectly still. He fell into a deep trance right in front of the giant poster of Manhattan that was on the wall. The poster seemed to come alive with the buildings swaying from side to side.

Lynton Viñas and Beowulf Perez: Demon Slayers in the Taal Inferno

Then, Sarafina stared menacingly at Lynton, who did not flinch but stared back with intensity. The nakedness made her feel liberated and she called out to Elashabab, "I am naked now, but I shall face you with swords tempered of fire and steel that will pierce your heart like a hot knife slicing through butter. Get ready for battle beast!"

Lynton Posing for the Cover of One of Wayne Frye's Books with Two Swords Rumoured to be Forged of Kryptonite to Fight Demons

Lynton Viñas and Beowulf Perez: Demon Slayers in the Taal Inferno

Lynton heard the mournful cry of a baby outside the front door. She slowly turned her head toward the door and stared. Was it a trick the demon was playing? Was there something sinister behind that cry? When dealing with demons, one had to be eternally vigilant.

Sarafina scornfully said, "Babies cry for the embrace of the devil. I shall take the soul of the little one now as it is easy to take that which has not been exposed to constant church propaganda. Little souls do not know it but they long for the warm embrace of the mighty sons of Cain, so that they might enjoy the magnificence and grandeur that comes from the exercise of pure evil." Then, Sarafina moved toward the door, but as Father Vasquez and Sarafina's parents stood by the door shaking in fear, Lynton just curled her lips smiling.

Lynton opened the door, and the woman, sitting there nursing the child looked up in shock at the naked Lynton standing before her. Lynton said, "Be gone and heed my advice. Stay away from this house until further notice."

Lynton Viñas and Beowulf Perez:
Demon Slayers in the Taal Inferno

There came a diabolical laugh from Sarafina as the deep voice said, "Ha, you think that you can save people from me. People love evil. Look at the greed in the world. People will do anything for money."

Then, slowly Sarafina's face became contorted and large pock marks appeared on her checks with green slime oozing out of them as she continued her oration of evil. "I could buy the baby's soul from the mother. She would sell it for a few thousand pesos to buy food that is only readily available to those with the money to buy it. Everything is for sale in a world based on greed. Go to Wall Street and find a man who is not obsessed with greed. Go to the seats of government here in this country and find a politician who does not first serve himself before others. Go to the churches that beg the poor to fill the collection plates so the Bishops can ride in chauffeured limousines and dine on caviar. Capitalism was invented by my lord and great master, Satan, who sits on the throne of greed. Capitalism brings us souls like a raging Tsunami roaring ashore to destroy everything in its path."

Lynton turned back and closed the door. She looked over at Father Vasquez and said, "Yes, I know that the church is more corporation than saviour of souls.

Lynton Viñas and Beowulf Perez: Demon Slayers in the Taal Inferno

Yes, I know that those on Wall Street would step over their own mothers to fuel their greed. Yes, politicians are the lowest life form on earth. Yet, within the hearts of the poor and downtrodden beats a spirit of hope, love and compassion for their fellow man. Among the poor you find grace and good will. Among the poor you find the will to share what they have with their neighbours. You want souls; go to the arrogant rich, because you already own their souls. They sacrifice all for their corrupt love of money. Theirs is an existence predicated on what they can procure materially not spiritually. I adhere to the profound teachings of a great man who once said to the rich man – give all you have to the poor. I could live in luxury, but I chose to live among the poor, because that is where I feel at home. The rich have nothing to offer but their own ego gratification. They have money but they are empty inside. The real treasure is not in the bank, the home you own or the car you drive. Real treasure lies within your heart. That is where true wealth dwells."

Pointing at her with anger, Sarafina waved her hand and Lynton fell to the floor. "You are mine, bitch!"

Lynton Viñas and Beowulf Perez:
Demon Slayers in the Taal Inferno

When Lynton was a child suckling on her mother's breast, her eyes twinkled and her mother felt a power within the child, as if the nourishment was not just for the body, but for the soul. Now, her mother was a woman who professed faith, but often was bereft of it when push came to shove. Lynton, on the other hand, never sought sanction from the church, because she had an inner strength that seemed to glisten and glow as if heaven gave her as a gift to the world, a gift that could shine the light of hope on those who had none.

As she lay on the floor, she summoned all her power as Sarafina stared down upon her with eyes burning with the fire of hell. Lynton's perfectly symmetrical breasts heaved up and down in a synchronized symphony of assuredness as she slowly rose and despite a whirlwind seeming to push her back, she fought against it as in the far corner Beowulf was slowly coming out of his comatose-like state.

Suddenly, a demon, as dark as death and many little demons, appeared in the far corner. They seemed to move toward Lynton, not in a walk, but a steady, even gliding motion as if they were floating on air. Sarafina in a low whisper said, "They are coming for you, coming to devour your soul, bitch. Get ready for the embrace of death. You are a woman doomed as is your despicable friend. You cannot defeat me."

Lynton Viñas and Beowulf Perez:
Demon Slayers in the Taal Inferno

Lynton stood tall, put out her right hand toward the demons in a stopping motion and said, as Beowulf looked on in disbelief. "Stop you figments of my mind. I know you are not real. You are a manifestation of evil that I rebuke."

Sarafina, laughing sinisterly said, "You stupid bitch. You do not know fact from fiction!"

With envy and anger the evil within Sarafina endured the hole in the dark abode that was now its home. Lynton was a woman of hope and whether the demon was real or a manifestation brought forth by Sarafina's powerful mind, Lynton was the epitome of fearlessness in the battle against evil. The sun and the moon were hers to command and they bowed before her light of goodness. It was as if she had heard each day the din of revel high the plucking harps of hope playing tunes of glory in the fields of grandeur. There was a triumphant air as she rose to once again stare down the evil intentions. It was as if she had become the all mighty and the fairest of fields enfolded by water, sun and moon were hers to command. She was fearless!

Sarafina moved steadily backwards as Lynton stared deeply into those evil fiery eyes. Each step forward brought an equal step backwards by Sarafina. This was a war, a war for the soul of Sarafina. Whether the entity was real or just manufactured within the mind, it was real to all those present. There was a monster inside her mind that was grim and determined. It might all be Sarafina's imagination that was producing sounds and kinetic powers that allowed her to levitate and to use energy to force others to bend to her will. Yet, none of that mattered, because whatever was happening could still destroy Sarafina's mind. There was a monster demon inside her causing a nightmare of despair, but the demon slayer was on the job.

Lynton Viñas and Beowulf Perez:
Demon Slayers in the Taal Inferno

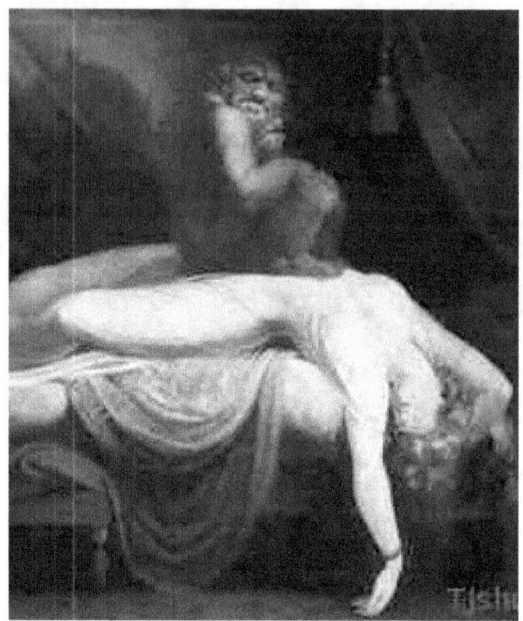

The Nightmare by Henry Fuseli

J. Wayne Frye

CHAPTER 3
MIGHTY WARRIOR INTO THE LION'S DEN

Evil on a night like this
Evil tasting like a twisted wish
Evil lying upon the ground
Evil feels the tears of fear
Evil tainted sounds of cheer
Evil dripping down in search of hate
Evil tearing down helpless fate
Evil swears that by the night's end
Evil won't say it was all pretend
Evil will stalk you
Evil until full content
Evil pleasured to full extent

Episode II

The night ended with all present exhausted from what they had seen. Sarafina fell into deep slumber after saying she recalled nothing that happened. Lynton, carefully putting her clothes back on with no sense of false modesty looked over at Father Vasquez who was apparently enjoying looking at her nakedness. His lechery elicited a smile from Lynton as she said, "There are books you can buy Father that have lots of naked women in them. I promise not to tell the Pope."

Somewhat taken aback by her frankness, he said, "I saw no need for your nakedness in front of all of us."

"It was necessary Father to show complete contempt for the entity. Modesty about nakedness is something we are taught by those who fear the human body, when it should be glorified and exalted."

"Poppycock, original sin led to nakedness being frowned upon," replied Father Vasquez.

"I was not in the Garden of Eden, and I committed no sin. I think it unfair to expect me to pay for the sins of others. I believe the church would be better served by worrying about poverty and injustice."

"The Catholic Church cannot be questioned. It is beyond rebuke. It is totally sacrosanct in all its dealings. "

Lynton Viñas and Beowulf Perez:
Demon Slayers in the Taal Inferno

"Anybody and anything can be questioned. Father, if there is a God he gave me a brain to use, not let it atrophy by allowing others to do my thinking for me. You called me in to help this woman, and now you dare question my methods? I am not here to serve the church. I and my friend are here to serve the needs of a woman who is either genuinely possessed by a demon, or at least thinks she is possessed. Either there is a demon or at least she believes there is a demon which makes her use a highly developed brain to manifest things that would appear out of the realm most of us understand. I am a sceptic despite the fact that others call me a demon fighter. What I have seen and what I have heard has led me to believe there are things beyond the realm of our understanding, but I still am not sure whether I believe in demons or not. However, I do believe in evil, especially the evil of man. Needless wars and unmitigated greed have convinced me that the greatest demon of all is mortal man. However, what we witnessed tonight is either truly a demon within this young woman, or it is her own mind playing tricks on her and, in the process, toying with our minds, making us see things that do not exist. I am going to battle this evil regardless and hopefully come out triumphant."

She looked at Beowulf and said, "Are you ready to do this my friend?"

"I am prepared to go into hell itself if necessary," he forcefully replied.

"It may be well be necessary my friend Beowulf, for I sincerely believe we either must enter her tortured mind and convince her we are going to slay this demon or that we will traverse that trail that leads to the place of evil where she either saw or manifested the demon. We may have to go into the fires of Taal and wrestle with the demon dragon she saw in reality or in her mind. It will be a dangerous journey, whichever we do."

She then turned to Darlene and Richard, "May we stay the night with you?"

"Of course," replied Darlene. "It is a humble home, but all we have is yours."

Lynton Viñas and Beowulf Perez:
Demon Slayers in the Taal Inferno

"Humble is the true stately palace, for humble is truly, without doubt, where compassion develops, grows, is nurtured and genuinely abides," interjected Beowulf.

Went they forth on a pallet laid on the floor in the humble home of those who endure the misery caused by capitalism where all the good is acquired on the backs of those who toil for miniscule rewards so the exalted at the top may cavort about in their finery and live in splendorous luxury. This abode had served the God of the Catholic Church in devotion, as the poor are told that after death they will get what they were denied in this life and walk streets in heaven paved with gold. It is what they cling to in a world where they are denied that to which all should be entitled – shelter, a job, medical care. Evil was already in the homes of the wealthy, but it was not satisfied with the people who had sold their souls for riches, as for some reason it took greater delight in dwelling within those who had so little. Perhaps that was the real mark of evil, the real sign of its insidious intents. It took delight in destroying that which had already had life reduced to a constant struggle to keep from sinking, sinking ever deeper into the quagmire of poverty.

Be it produced by a furtive mind or be it a real demon rising from the fiery pits of the mighty Taal, sweet Sarafina was fast asleep after feasting in fearful sorrow on the evil that was working tirelessly for her soul. Unhallowed, grim and greedy, the demon of her mind grasp the reckless, wrathful evil that had found a resting place within her. The demon was real regardless of whether it was a physical entity or not, for it had found a resting place for its spoil of hatred and venomous malcontent where it wanted to slaughter the soul of a good and decent young woman.

Lynton arose quickly, looked around the room and realized that she had not explored the reasons for this malady. She had been so wrapped up in the events that transpired she had overlooked that which might lend a clue to why this girl had been visited with this nightmare. She awakened Beowulf and said, "Come, we have no time to lose. I must talk to Father Vasquez.

J. Wayne Frye

Lynton Viñas and Beowulf Perez:
Demon Slayers in the Taal Inferno

Now, ironically, Beowulf was reluctant to arise, for he had been lying there thinking of Lynton in all her naked glory. His arousal asserting itself had kept him from slumber as he kept thinking of the beauty of her soft brown skin that glistened delightfully in the flickering candle light of the humble home. He looked sheepishly at Lynton and sighed.

Lynton said, "Come on Beowulf, we must get the answer to a question now."

Beowulf, still embarrassed that Lynton might notice his arousal, could not help but look upon her angelic face and succulent lips that appeared to always be begging for a kiss. Gazing upon her gorgeous pouty lips that were sensuously puffy and seemingly puckered for carnal delight, he determinedly bowed his head to avoid looking and continuing his aroused state.

Lynton, used to men fawning over her, and unabashedly aware of most men's seemingly uncontrollable urges for carnal pleasure said, "Cool it Beo, I'm spoken for, but I appreciate the interest. It is a compliment for a handsome man like you to be aroused by little old demure me, but it ain't gonna happen. I'm spoken for and devoted to my Wayne. So, zip it up, corral it down and let's go."

Never had Beowulf been so dramatically and irrevocably told no. Ironically, even that refusal made him more aroused by this little thing called the dynamic dynamo. He got himself moderately under control and smiled as he crawled off the pallet that had been spread on the floor for him. "Ready demon fighter."

They laughed uproariously together and headed toward the church. Beowulf asked her what she needed to ask Father Vasquez that couldn't wait, but she simply said, "Wait and be bedazzled by the astuteness of the dynamic dynamo."

Again they laughed together, and at that moment the camaraderie between the two was solidified into a mutual bond of respect. Still, Beowulf could not help but trail slightly behind her to cut his eyes downward to observe that gorgeous wiggle in the tight fitting

Lynton Viñas and Beowulf Perez:
Demon Slayers in the Taal Inferno

shorts that moulded so magnificently around the most curvaceously perfect derriere he had ever seen. If the hand of God made each of us, he thought to himself, wow, he must have worked overtime when he got down there on little old Lynton. Michelangelo himself could not have sculpted a more perfectly shaped butt. It was truly a work of art.

Lynton, realizing what was happening, just ignored it, as she learned long ago that men were the most ridiculous creatures to ever inhabit the earth. Even her dear older, supposedly more mature Wayne loved going to a place called Watson's Drugstore, which was notorious for its beautiful women clerks who roamed about the aisles in short skirts and high heels. "Men, she thought – can't live with them, can't live without them."

Father Vasquez groggily got out of the tiny cubicle where he slept in the back of the small church. The late night pounding on the door was not all that unusual as occasionally parishioners would come to the church for help with domestic problems at a late hour. Ironically, he, too, had found himself in deep thought about Lynton who had not yielded to what he thought was his authority as a priest. She had stood up to him, and even pointedly called him out for lechery of sorts. He was a priest, but that did not mean he checked his libido into hiatus when he accepted the collar. He was a man, and he had to admit that there was something about Lynton that titillated him in a way that he thought had been relegated to his past.

The two late night interlopers heard the bolt on the door being pulled aside, and Lynton thought how ironic that a church had to be locked to keep people out. With homeless people sleeping on the streets, empty pews would make nice beds and the church would offer protection from the elements. She found it ironic that a place that preached compassion could not use simple logic to practice that which it preached.

Still groggy, Father Vasquez said, "My, it is so late. Is there something wrong?"

Lynton apologetically replied, "I am sorry to awaken you Father, but there is a question that must be answered immediately. "In the past, have there been other incidents like the one Sarafina is experiencing now."

Sighing, he replied, "Yes, there have been two others that ended tragically." He stepped back from the door and motioned for them to enter. They moved to a back pew and all three took a seat as he continued: "About four years ago, a young boy, well young to me. He was 14 when he began a radical transformation. He was a reverential and devoted person here in the church, and one day I came into the sanctuary unnoticed and found him at the altar doing an unspeakable act."

Lynton looked directly at the Father, who was obviously too embarrassed or too repressed to use the word, but she said, "Masturbating."

Bowing his head and letting out a deep sigh, he said, "Yes, I am afraid so. And what was even worse, he turned to me without stopping and laughed, and in a voice similar to the one used by Sarafina said, "Join me, Father?"

Lynton Viñas and Beowulf Perez: Demon Slayers in the Taal Inferno

"A perfectly natural act for an adolescent, but I am not sure the church is the proper place to do it," offered Lynton. Then she continued. "Let me guess. This happened after he had made a trek to the caldera of the volcano."

"Yes," replied a surprised Father Vasquez.

"And he met a tragic end?"

"Yes."

"No doubt at the volcano. He disappeared on a trek to the caldera?"

Surprised at her perceptiveness, Father Vasquez simply nodded his head affirmatively. Taking a deep breath, Lynton asked, "And the other incident?"

"It happened almost ten years ago now. Another young girl same age as Sarafina. She too was a loyal devotee to our lord and saviour, Jesus Christ, but a change came over her at times that turned her into a wanton harlot who foisted herself on young and old men in the village one day, and the next she was a meek and dutiful servant of our lord."

"The change in demeanour occurred after a trek to Taal?"

"Right."

"And again her end came in exactly the same manner as the boy's. She disappeared on the mountain."

"Yes, yes. But she left a note. It simply said that she was going into pit to embrace Elashabab."

Lynton got up and said, "Thank you so mush Father Vasquez. This is going to be more difficult than I imagined, and time is of the essence, as we have little of it. There is a full moon coming in two days, and on the night of the next full moon she is going to make a trek up Taal. My guess is that these manifestations always lasted 4 months right, and on the full moon of the fourth month, the other two disappeared."

Lynton Viñas and Beowulf Perez: Demon Slayers in the Taal Inferno

Father Vasquez nodded his head up and down as he said, "Yes, four months exactly, but I am not sure of the full moon."

"Get the dates of their deaths tomorrow Father, and give them to Beo." She then turned to Beowulf and said, "Go to the library in Tagaytay and check the dates to see if there were not full-moons on the dates of the deaths."

Father Vasquez emphatically said, "No need to wait until tomorrow my friends. I will check the church registry for their death dates right now."

He quickly went into the vestry. There were the sounds of drawers being opened and papers being shuffled. He returned promptly, handing the dates to Beowulf.

Father Vasquez and Lynton would never be great friends as they looked at life so differently, but they were gaining mutual respect for one another. Lynton and Beowulf left, and as they walked back to the Sanchez home, Lynton just shook her head and purposefully walked in front of Beowulf, looked over her shoulders and said, "You men. You saw it naked, but are more excited watching it wiggling in my shorts. I will never understand the mind of a man."

The two were developing great simpatico and respect. Still Lynton could not help but laugh at Beo's obsession with her butt. Then again, her Wayne was obsessed with it too. She giggled to herself as she thought that, well; maybe it is pretty nice after all.

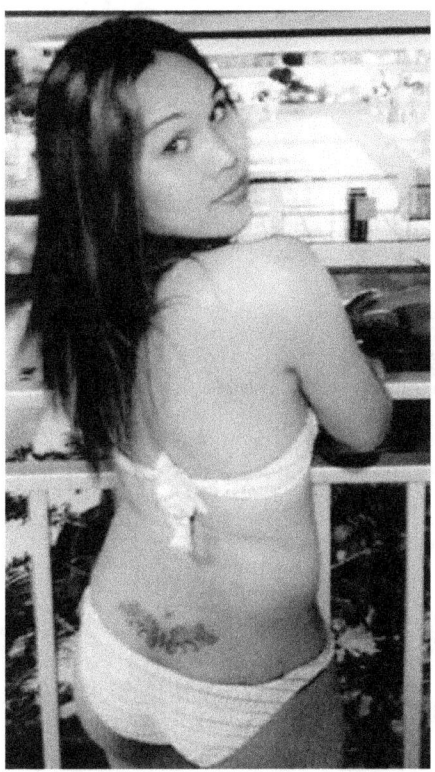

Photo of What Fascinated Beowulf

Lynton Viñas and Beowulf Perez:
Demon Slayers in the Taal Inferno

At the dawning of day, Beowulf took a boat back to Taygaytay to find out about the full moon dates, as the internet on the island was provided by Globe Communications, which was notorious for poor service. Poor Filipinos thought Lynton, who had spent time in Canada, the USA and Asian countries, where internet companies were held to a much higher standard than they were in the Philippines where slow download and upload speeds were standard fare unless you paid exorbitant fees that only the rich could afford. Like everything else in the world of capitalism, all good things were reserved only for those at the top. As she waited for Beowulf's return, she took a stroll with Sarafina to school so that she could develop better rapport with her.

As they walked, Lynton began to probe her inner most thoughts. "So, Sarafina, how do you feel about what lies ahead for you? Are you excited about going to university?"

"I am, yes, very much so. I will be the first in my family, and I do not want to let them down. They are very proud of me for my hard work and dedication, but

Lynton Viñas and Beowulf Perez: Demon Slayers in the Taal Inferno

I know they are distraught over what has happened to me. Believe me, Ms. Viñas, I have no recollection of the things I say and do when in that horrible state, but I have heard about it from my siblings. I am so ashamed."

Very deliberately, Lynton said, "My name is Lynton, please. And always remember that the voice of intelligence is drowned out by the roar of fear. It is ignored by the voice of desire. It is contradicted by the voice of shame. It is biased by hate and extinguished by anger. Most of all it is silenced by ignorance. You are not ignorant my dear – far from it. You will lick this thing, and I am here to help you do it."

Sarafina smiled broadly and touched Lynton's arm. "Thank you so much."

They stopped at the school grounds. Suddenly a look of fierceness manifested itself in Sarafina's countenance. Her eyes became like daggers ready to pierce the heart of an enemy. In a coarse, deep voice she said, "I'll eat you heart and liver bitch as I dine at the table of my master Satan. I spit upon your sanctimonious belief in good. I deplore good as I deplore you, bitch."

Eyes of Fire Displayed by Sarafina

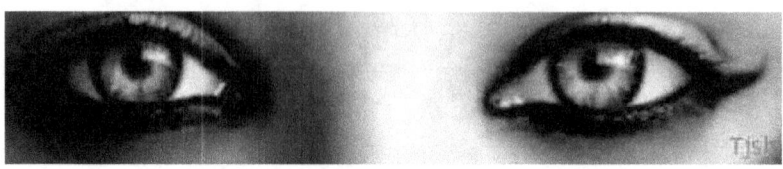

Lynton not intimidated or surprised, very calmly replied. "I look forward to our battle Elashabab. I may put on my high heels from hell and kick your ass. Have a good day." She turned and walked away, not looking back as the entity mumbled some obscenities that were unintelligible. This would be a battle like no other Lynton ever faced, and she was actually unsure of what fate awaited her, Beowulf and Sarafina. At this point, her assuredness was more act than fact.

A review of data with Beowulf confirmed the disappearances were at full-moon. She left with Beowulf to get some props that would be used to confront the entity or Sarafina who was manifesting the entity in her mind. Beowulf went with her to visit a man who forged ancient combat weapons where they purchased battle garb as Lynton explained that it was essential to confront this thing as if it was a battle between good and evil in the ancient tradition, because modern weapons were useless against this type of manifestation of mind or demon.

She had Beowulf return to the library to do research on Elashabab while she went back to the island. Later in the day when Sarafina came home from school there were no appearances of the entity and what had happened earlier in the day at school was not mentioned as Sarafina would have had no relocation of the event, so Lynton saw no need to burden her with worry. Sarafina seemed curious about the large trunk that was delivered, but Lynton said it was just things she and Beowulf needed from home as they were staying awhile.

The might of Elashabab was shared with Lynton by Beowulf who had thoroughly researched the demon at the Tagaytay Library. It seems that many souls were purportedly lost to the demon over the years, all from an area on a map shared by Beowulf. Near what is known as the decade volcanoes because of their ferocity and potential for cataclysmic devastation, many reports of people being possessed by the demons Elashabab and Abbaddon had surfaced. The Catholic Church had made a concentrated effort to cover up the details, because the rumoured 47 possessions had led to the deaths of three priests who unsuccessfully tried to perform exorcisms. Their deaths included one decapitation, one brain haemorrhage so violent the head exploded and one heart being ripped from the body.

Each place was designated by scientists as areas where cataclysmic earthquakes were likely to occur at almost anytime. Rumblings of the volcanoes all coincided with tales of demonic possessions, and as far as Beowulf could determine, those who were possessed all mysteriously disappeared, some even having been seen walking toward the volcanoes.

Lynton, ever the sceptic said, "So, volcanic activity followed by indications of demonic possession. Is it not true that religion used to promote volcanoes as the rumblings of Satan in hell?

"Yes, that is true."

Lynton Viñas and Beowulf Perez:
Demon Slayers in the Taal Inferno

Taal Volcano in Tagaytay, Philippines

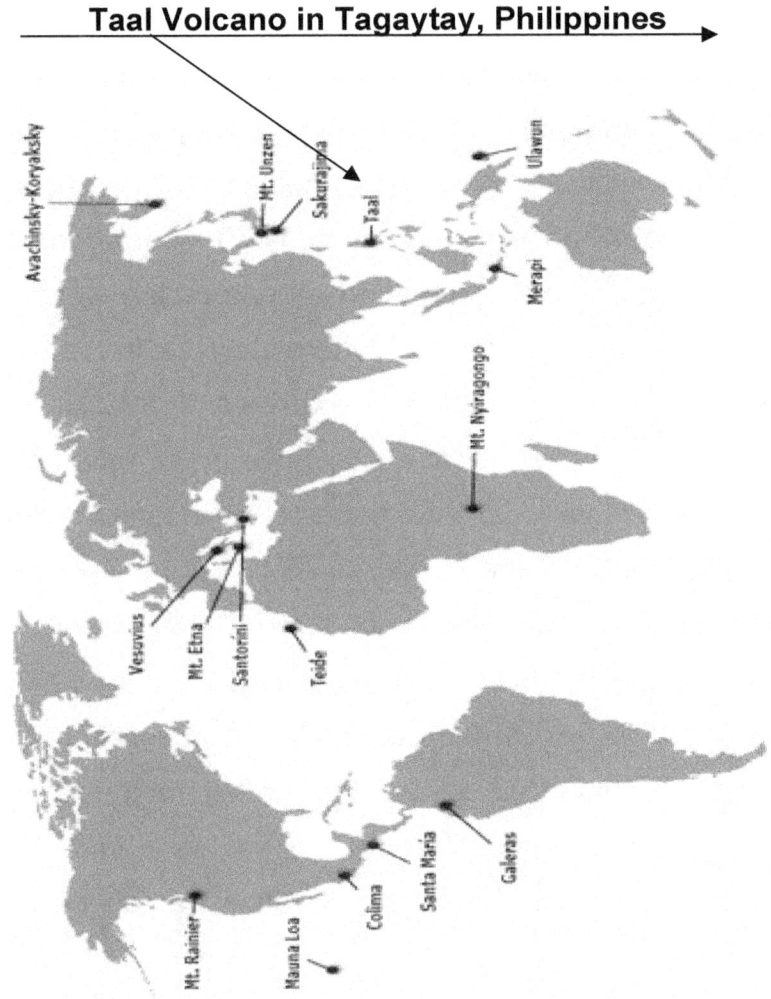

Then it could all be the power of suggestion?"

"I suppose that is possible, replied Beowulf.

Smiling, Lynton said, I suppose all things are possible."

Lynton Viñas and Beowulf Perez:
Demon Slayers in the Taal Inferno

Beowulf began a stoic discourse on the two demons that inhabit volcanoes. "Abbaddon and Elashabab have been known for thousands of years as the demons of fire that manifest themselves as dragons when not inhabiting a human body. They are demons of lore that have meandered all across the world to burning volcanic infernos where they lie in wait for souls that they want to conquer and trap in the inferno. The past decade they have been reported in 16 different venues, all of them being decade volcano areas which when they erupt will bring vast devastation."

At that point, Lynton, formulating a question in her mind for the Father, said, "Wait and tell me the rest as we go to Father Vasquez for a very important question. I think I know why Sarafina was chosen as the third victim here, but I need some clarification from Father Vasquez."

The Father was excited to see the two, and uncharacteristically seemed gregarious. They went into the vestry and had a seat. Lynton said, "Father – the number 48. Tell me about it."

J. Wayne Frye

Lynton Viñas and Beowulf Perez:
Demon Slayers in the Taal Inferno

"Genesis 48, the number that represents the Father's Blessings. It is a number mocked by the devil, because he wanted no blessings from the Father."

Smiling, Lynton said, "And about four months ago you delivered a sermon about Genesis 48, calling it a sacred number that was mocked by the devil."

"Why yes, I would say it was about four months ago."

Sighing and licking her lips, Lynton said, "And Sarafina was in church that day, and she went to you and asked you more about the number and what it meant. Right?"

"Yes, she did indeed, but I fail to see what this has to do with what is happening to her."

"It has everything to do with it Father."

"You mean my sermon has something to do with the manifestation of the demon."

Lynton Viñas and Beowulf Perez:
Demon Slayers in the Taal Inferno

Nodding her head enthusiastically, she said, "She also asked about the demons Elashabab and Abbaddon did she not?"

"She did, and I told her about how they inhabit active volcanoes before rising from the fire to seek souls."

Sighing again, Lynton asked another question. "Do you know if she researched these demons? Did she ever ask for information on them or journey where she might find out about them in some library?"

"I don't recall her asking about them, no. I do, however, remember her asking to go with me to the seminary in Dasmarinas so she could visit the library there. Perhaps she did do some research while there. I would not know as I was tied up with the Bishop all day."

"Oh, she did some research alright, and she found out that the church has recorded 47 incidents of possession in places near decade volcanoes, including Taal. You see, she is the 48th possession in a line that runs from Seattle all across Europe and Asia until it reaches Taal."

Confused, Father Vasquez murmured, "Decade volcanoes?"

"Decade Volcanoes are 16 volcanoes identified as being worthy of particular study in light of their history of large, destructive eruptions and proximity to populated areas. They are likely to violently explode at any time."

"And you believe she studied about this and convinced herself of what?"

"Father, I am a sceptic about all things. As I have said, if there is a God, he gave us a brain to use, not let atrophy. I question everything with a healthy scepticism, and I believe Sarafina is a sceptic too, but she became fascinated with how demonic possessions were being reported around areas in proximity to these 16 decade volcanoes. The number 48 is significant, because she would be the 48th victim of possession. She wants to be a believer, but she has doubts that she is fearful of revealing. I am not questioning the likelihood she is possessed or that there might well be demons involved here, because I have faced many demons in my life, the worst being the kind that are walking the streets with us every day. The demons of ignorance, poverty and greed are abominable evils that we all must face in a world run by the few for the benefit of the few. Sarafina is not ignorant, but she does live in an isolated village where questioning the church is frowned upon. She has a very active mind that may well be susceptible to illusionary manifestations."

Beowulf and Father Vasquez were amazed at Lynton's depth of knowledge. She continued, "The might of these two demons is well-known, and 47 victims are already in their graves presumably; although, my guess is that none of their bodies were ever found. Am I correct?"

"As far as I know, that is correct."

"There were no bodies, because they all went into the caldera of the volcanoes."

J. Wayne Frye

Lynton Viñas and Beowulf Perez:
Demon Slayers in the Taal Inferno

Shaking his head, Father Vasquez said, "Oh no, no, it can't be, absolutely not possible that all those people would walk to their deaths knowingly."

"Oh yes father, it can be and is. These people walked to their doom on Taal and the other places, all led by their own hallucinations or by those demons. I am not sure which, but I intend to find out. The two others here in the village who were possessed, their names please."

"Yes, yes, I understand completely. I do. The first was Charlotte Ramirez and then there was John Venar."

"Will you come with us immediately please Father Vasquez? Time is of the essence. I need to talk with their parents."

"Yes, of course," he said as he arose and pointed toward the door.

Beowulf looked at Lynton, and he had never seen such beauty and determination.

Lynton Viñas and Beowulf Perez: Demon Slayers in the Taal Inferno

A worried Lynton as she was leaving the vestry.

The church as it appeared in their minds when they looked back at it.

As they left the church, they all, for some reason, felt overwhelmingly compelled to look back at the church, and as they did so it appeared to be upside down to all three of them. Father Vasquez and Beowulf were startled, but Lynton said, "Do not look back my friends. Look to the left at that figure over by the donkey stables."

There staring at them was Sarafina. They were too far away to see the expression on her face. One did not have to see what was obvious though. There was, no doubt, an evil grin. Lynton said, "She is playing with our minds. Come on, we have work to do."

They called on the parents of the first victim, Charlotte Ramirez. Both bowed humbly before Father Vasquez as if he was the Pope himself. He introduced them and said, "They are trying to help Sarafina, and need your cooperation."

They readily offered to do all they could, and Lynton said, "Your daughter appeared to be possessed for four months and one day she just disappeared. Did anyone see her walking toward Taal?"

Ms. Ramirez said, "Perhaps, one neighbour said she saw her walking passed the stables which are at the base of the trail to Taal. It was dark, of course, so she was never sure, but she always felt it was her."

Lynton Viñas and Beowulf Perez:
Demon Slayers in the Taal Inferno

"And she left home around 3:33 AM, right?

"Yes, I suppose as that is about the time she was seen by the stables."

"Did you ever see her scribble the number 999 on anything in the house or maybe in some of her notebooks from school?"

Mr. Ramirez got up and eagerly walked over to a dilapidated, dusty old bookshelf and removed a spiral notebook. He handed it to Lynton and there was page after page with the number 999, 999, 999 scribbled on them.

Lynton then asked another question, though she knew the answer. "Was Charlotte extremely smart, probably the smartest one on her class?"

"Yes," replied Ms. Ramirez, "Always at the top of her class."

"Finally, did you ever see a pentagram anywhere in the house?"

J. Wayne Frye

Quizzically, both Ramirez's replied at the same time, "Pentagram?"

"A five-pointed star drawn under a bed or maybe in a corner of a room?"

"Yes, she had drawn one under her bed," replied Mr. Ramirez.

Lynton got up and said, "Thank you so much. You have been very helpful."

They left and went to John Venar's parents' home where Lynton asked the same questions and got the exact same answers. Then, mystified as they left, Beowulf and Father Vasquez begged to know what all this was leading up to. Lynton, as they walked back toward Sarafina's home said, "Evil is based on numbers. Three is the first sacred number, the first perfect number for evil intentions. Three represents the pagan trinity. You know that Father Vasquez."

Nodding his head yes, he replied, "Of course. Yes I do."

Lynton Viñas and Beowulf Perez:
Demon Slayers in the Taal Inferno

"Then, you know it is represented geometrically in the triangle, and spiritually as the Third Eye of Hinduism. Occultists will multiply and add three to other sacred numbers to create new numbers. However, they also group threes in two's and threes, because they believe in the principle of intensification so that greater power is achieved when a sacred number is grouped. In the case of three, greater intensification is achieved when it is shown as 33, or 333. 333 + 333 equals 666. Notice, in all likelihood both girls left home at 3:33 AM. Occultists have used 333 as the hidden symbol by which they present the much more offensive number 666. When the details of an event are so arranged as to contain certain sacred occult numbers or numeric combinations, this is literally a stealth occult signature on the event. Mathematically speaking, 666 can be created when three pairs of threes are added. Thus, (3+3) + (3+3) + (3+3) = 666, which is the sign of the beast, the anti-Christ."

As Beowulf and Father Vasquez sat mystified by her knowledge, Lynton continued. "Nine is sacred because it is the "first cube of an odd number (3). The

Lynton Viñas and Beowulf Perez:
Demon Slayers in the Taal Inferno

triple nine (999) is utilized to represent 666, because it is simply the inversion of 666."

Father Vasquez was mesmerized by the detail Lynton was using to describe the incredible power of numbers in the manifestation of evil. His jaw dropped and you could almost see the wheels turning in his mind as this extraordinarily knowledgeable woman laid out the foundation for what was occurring in the Sanchez home.

Beowulf, also fascinated that someone who seemed to be highly suspicious of religion and was, at best, an agonistic, could be so thoroughly versed in the Bible and the occult. Lynton simply was an academic thinker who knew the value of research in ferreting out the truth. He admiringly asked, "What then is your hypothesis?"

"All three victims here in this village were abnormally obsessed or maybe possessed by numbers that represented evil. Plain to see that there is something very sinister at work here, and it could be that three very smart girls simply had, or in

Lynton Viñas and Beowulf Perez:
Demon Slayers in the Taal Inferno

Sarafina's case, has, active, furtive, imaginative minds. This is a baffling, mystifying and intriguing series of circumstances that may be mass hallucinations and/or hypnotically induced states of catatonic manifestations."

They walked together but one of them walked with more determination than the others. Beowulf looked at Lynton and he imagined a mighty warrior about to walk into the lion's den of evil with sword and shield to battle the demons of darkness. An intense image of Lynton Viñas, warrior, started to manifest itself in his mind as they marched onward to meet their fate.

Image of Lynton in Beowulf's Mind

CHAPTER 4
GO AND MEET YOUR FATE

I execute evil to preserve the righteous.

I am Lynton Viñas, demon slayer.

In my hand I hold the universe.

I have the power to attack evil.

The preservation of the righteous is my goal.

So, I slay evil with the polished steel

On the dagger that I wield unmercifully.

My eyes see through deceit and mockery.

My voice shakes the earth, the moon and the stars.

I embrace the world of light

And slay the darkness.

Lynton Viñas and Beowulf Perez:
Demon Slayers in the Taal Inferno

There are those who labour tirelessly for justice and Lynton Viñas was one of those people. She was now on the trail of a fiend of mind, the volcano or both. She was tracing the fear as she had seen the loathsomeness of the evil that was wrecking young lives. The unrighteous ruled a world based on greed where the most loathsome of men sit like grand potentates on thrones of gold without a thought for those they trampled in satisfaction of their immoral pursuit of more and more. The minds of the righteous were afflicted as they were playthings for devils and demons that danced and cavorted about looking for more and more souls to corral in their den of inequity.

Lynton knew not whether it was all manufactured in Sarafina's mind or that perhaps there was truly something evil within the fires of Taal. The point was, no matter which, Sarafina was in mortal danger as had been proven by the 47 others who had met their demise. There were sorrows a plenty in the little village at the base of the volcano, and Lynton and Beowulf had the power to address at least a bit of that sorrow. For ten years since the first incident, there came hidden tidings of evil that danced merrily about

J. Wayne Frye

Lynton Viñas and Beowulf Perez:
Demon Slayers in the Taal Inferno

the village waiting for the right time to snatch another victim to complete the cycle of 48. That was the magic number that somehow would unleash a cataclysmic rumbling of the 16 volcanoes that would indeed rock the world.

Unearthly tidings are common in places where superstition holds sway. There had long been tales of the demons of fire that lived in Taal, and that periodically they spat out devastation to remind mortals that they had no power over them. The last large eruption was in 1977, and three people were actually killed when they made an offering to quell the demons in the caldera. They fell to their deaths, or as some said, the demons claimed them.

Why one wonders do people live at the base of a volcano, but for the few people who called the village home, the volcano, as a tourist attraction, was their livelihood, a way to put rice on bare tables. Many had died over the years and the fear of the beasts in the caldera was unfading to the villagers. The evil there was real to them as they felt dogged by it. It haunted them day and night as horrors were heaped upon

Lynton Viñas and Beowulf Perez:
Demon Slayers in the Taal Inferno

them by what they thought were demons on thrones of fire. The Almighty they depended on, but their lives were really ruled by the dooms-men of deeds that sat within the burning fires of Taal. It was woe for the villagers who in harm and hatred had their souls clutched in fiery embraces.

From this point on, it must be stated that what occurred can not be independently verified for the most part. Whether what occurred actually happened in reality or just in the minds of the participants this author cannot say as can any of those who participated in the events about to be described. Still, what occurred did have profound results on the lives of all there.

Episode III

There was seething hatred building within Sarafina as the demons of her mind began to take over. The woe of these days played a symphony of misery for her parents. Lynton and Beowulf, the wisest of humans, assuaged sorrow; soothed the anguish, loathly and long, that lay on these good folks. Their

Lynton Viñas and Beowulf Perez:
Demon Slayers in the Taal Inferno

baneful burdens were eased knowing that two mighty valorous warriors were in their midst. Lynton's name had been known in the village for a long time as it was near there in Taygaytay that her famous adventure *Lynton Walks on Water*, which was recorded for posterity by Wayne Frye, made her a household name. She was a battle queen in the minds of the villagers, ready to fight against forces of evil as she had done so many times before.

Lynton Viñas and Beowulf Perez:
Demon Slayers in the Taal Inferno

She bade Beowulf, as they walked into the humble abode of the Sanchez family, to assist her in making ready for battle. He stood in admiration now, somewhat overcoming his romantic inclinations, though his libido still would not allow him to turn his mind completely away from she who had sensuality like no woman he had ever seen before.

She looked at him with admiration and love and knew she had indeed chosen her comrade well. It was as if she were commanding a great ship with Beowulf as first mate. Together they were going to sail the sea of Sarafina's mind and confront Elashabab.

On board they climbed this ship of the deranged mind, ready, hope churning the sea with mighty waves; the two sailors bore on the breast of the bark their bright array, their weapons of steel being removed from the trunk. Then moved they over the waters by might of the wind that barks like a bird with breast of foam, until in season due, they saw with Sarafina whom they tied down to her bed, sea-cliffs evil in darkness shining on steep high hills, headlands broad.

J. Wayne Frye

Lynton Viñas and Beowulf Perez:
Demon Slayers in the Taal Inferno

They sent Sarafina's parents from the room along with Father Vasquez who would keep vigil with them. Warned that under no circumstances should they venture forth into the locked room, Lynton and Beowulf prepared for the ultimate confrontation between good and evil, putting their battle garb on.

In regal battle armour, the two stood almost naked to hide nothing. Sarafina started spitting out green slime as she shouted obscenities at them so vile that Beowulf felt embarrassed that Lynton had to hear them. The names she called her were an abomination to someone so filled with goodness, but it did not seem to affect her at all as nearly naked she stood defiantly.

The two of them seemed to go into a deep trance and on a wind of terrible force the two were borne toward Taal. They were dropped into the dust at the bottom of the hill that led to the Crater Lake. Down then quickly the two descended.

Anchored down with shields and swords, the armour clashing for battle, now saw they the cliff at the base of the lake of fire. There was a gargoyle-like creature with wings on the far side down near the shore of the crater as if he were a warden watching for intruders. Wonder overwhelmed the gargoyle, looking as the clock of doom could be heard tolling 3:33 as suddenly overhead floated Sarafina descending gradually into the lake of fire.

In a booming voice, the dark, menacing gargoyle asked, "Who are you to ponder before the lake of fire? I, sentinel set over the lake here, lest any foe try to, without invitation breach this domain, warn you to halt before the great ruler of the underworld, Satan the Magnificent."

Lynton Viñas and Beowulf Perez:
Demon Slayers in the Taal Inferno

"I am Lynton Viñas, demon fighter, and this is my warrior friend, Beowulf. We come to fight for the soul of Sarafina Sanchez."

Raising its head and spitting fire, the gargoyle said, "Clearly you lack sanity to challenge the son of Belmoda. Do you not know Elashabab and his brother Abbaddon are about to unleash the greatest fury to ever befall mankind. This girl is the 48th victim who will assure the greatest destruction the world has ever known. Clearly you lack perspective here. I admit in you two I see the mightiest to have ever challenged these mighty lords of the underworld. A greater determination I have never seen in the eyes of any foe, but I tell you to return the sooner the better or you shall taste a death as never was imaginable. I shall rain fire and water upon you, steam of hell from my master Satan shall scald you into submission. Be not complacent in your assessment of the terror that awaits you. Go back before it is too late."

Episode IV

We hear you clearly but be assured that we know a

demon can be defeated. I carry tempered steel, as does my colleague, which was forged of kryptonite from the distant planet that once was home to mighty warriors who tried to settle here but found it too inhospitable. I seek to confront a scathing monster of deceit that you serve. I have walked on water, I have faced Belmoda and survived, and I have exposed charlatans of the church as I will now expose charlatans of Satan. I embrace this contest and desire to savour the blood of he who dares seek the soul of a young woman who had known no sin. If cure shall follow, and the evil of Taal should rise I shall cool it with fervour from my heart that is righteous."

"You woman are belligerent and shall face a battle like none you have ever encountered. You think two can defeat Elashabab? You woman shall suffer sorrow as you would not believe. This is not a game played by the timid. This is a game played for souls."

Lynton, still unbowed, as an admiring Beowulf looked on, said, "I march into his lair and spit in his eye. Step aside and allow the battle for a soul to be waged. You cannot contain my anger here outside the pit of despair. I shall only be appeased by the blood of the evil one, Elashabab. He appears as a dragon, and dragons can be slain at full moon. I am a dragon slayer come to spill the blood of the one who dares tread upon the sanctified scared ground that abounds within the home of Sarafina Sanchez. I shall stand triumphant against evil. Move I tell you. Move aside or you too will incur the wrath of Lynton Viñas, demon slayer!"

Impressed by her will, the sentinel said, "March, then, bearing your kryptonite forged weapons and determination, but it shall do you no good. Go in haste to your doom."

Down went they into the fiery pit, marching into the fiery red lake where they stopped and surveyed the scene. The gargoyle whispered behind them, "Find your way then to your doom. Go ye into hell."

They sunk into the dark red lake and without breath they went down and down until they arrived at a large dark cavern where the mucky water was only ankle deep. Suddenly Beowulf shook his head, looked at

Lynton Viñas and Beowulf Perez:
Demon Slayers in the Taal Inferno

Lynton and said, "Are we in a dream of Sarafina's mind? Is this real or are we, in reality, back at the Sanchez home, still in her bedroom with her tied to the bed?"

"I do not know. If this is a dream, it is a shared dream manifested by the mind of a girl whose prowess in the suggestive arts is like no other I have ever known. She is a powerful shaman if this is a dream, for I feel the water. I can sense the coming heat. Stick with me on this journey. Follow me Beowulf and we shall defeat this evil whether it is real or just of the mind."

His sexual arousal may have waned, but as a man, he could not help but notice her physical attributes that started at her dainty little feet, worked its way up to her beautifully turned ankles that led to muscular calves that were a forerunner to the thighs that bristled with seductiveness. Her not overly muscular abs were still as taut as an archer's bow and her small but perky breasts jutted out like two small mountain peaks standing tall and defiant. Her long, black hair cascaded over her shoulders' going half way down her athletically slightly broad shoulders. Oh, and her derriere was the stuff of legends!

Follow her he willingly did, and now, he, for reasons he did not comprehend, did not concentrate on her wiggle as she was nearly naked, but, rather, he concentrated on her determination with her long sword in hand; ready to slay a demon to save a soul.

Lynton Viñas and Beowulf Perez:
Demon Slayers in the Taal Inferno

Without trepidation Lynton trudged forward, never wavering in her determination until they came upon tormented souls writhing in pain only to then see others with hands reaching skyward as if to plead for divine intervention to ease their torment as they tumbled into the pit of despair.

Lynton Viñas and Beowulf Perez:
Demon Slayers in the Taal Inferno

Never deterred from her goal, Lynton looked upon that which lay before her and knew that one day others, and maybe even herself, might be there after death. She and Beowulf were free to roam, because they had not been captured by death yet, nor had Sarafina, whose soul was being pruned of all righteousness so that it could be claimed by the evil one. Despite the misery and the terrible wailing and gnashing of teeth that ground into the soul, the two looked upon the misery with compassion, but travelled ever onward. To their right, left, straight ahead and behind them were souls seething in misery. It was often so depressing that they both closed their eyes for a second to avoid seeing all the suffering.

Lynton Viñas and Beowulf Perez:
Demon Slayers in the Taal Inferno

Her eyes were fixed on what lay ahead. Erect,
she rose above the flame, great chest, great brow;
she seemed to hold all Hell in disrespect
As before her hope began to grow.

The climb sapped her strength, still she cried:
"Sweet Beowulf, turn to me: do not pause
Or you shall be left here on the mountainside!"

She pointed to a long curved ledge a little ahead
that wrapped around the whole face of the slope.
"Pull yourself that much higher, my friend," she said.

Her words so spurred him that he forced himself
to push on after her on hands and knees, though exhausted,
until at last his feet were resting firmly on that shelf.

She drew him as if she was wrapped in heaven's cloak,
and pulling him with words behind her, she sped on
over the water, over rock as light as any boat.

Nearing the far bank, he heard her say
in tones so sweet I cannot here call them back,
much less describe them: "we are free"

J. Wayne Frye

Lynton Viñas and Beowulf Perez:
Demon Slayers in the Taal Inferno

*Then, the sweet Lynton took his head between
her open arms, and embracing; she hugged him
and made him feel sanctified and clean.*

*Thus they had traversed through caverns of hell,
and now they stood strong and bold together
ready and determined not to fail.*

Episode V

Bright was the glow from Lynton as she forged ahead, a warrior proud and grim with determination. Her prowess as a righteous defender of those lost in hopelessness was well known even in the bowels of the earth where tormented souls floundered helplessly.

There were demons on all sides seething with intense anger that someone so boldly dare enter the netherworld in search of he whom they all adored and fondly worshipped just as they did Satan. There before her was the demon of temptation, Mara, who preyed upon people's minds to get them to submit to the whims of the flesh so that they might be primed and ready to be sacrificed to debaucheries' glory. He was a despicable demon who had been tossed from the path of the righteous by the angels of light when they found him engaging in heinous debauchery.

Mara – Demon of Temptation

Mara spoke to Lynton: "Hoary bitch, how dare you come into our lair in search of the great one." This demon's might of mind to all there was known, his heinousness was glorified by the foulest of demons. He spat mucky slime Lynton's way and she dodged it as he said, "He there by your side lusts for you."

Now Mara was a tempter, the one that had tempted Gautama Buddha by trying to seduce him with the vision of his beautiful daughters. Mara personified unwholesome impulses, un-skilfulness and the death of the spiritual life. He was a master at using attraction, delusion and sexual arousal to take over all thought and orient the mind toward obsession with debauchery. He was the very greatest of tempters, distracting humans from practicing the spiritual life by making mundane things seem alluring, or the negative seem positive.

There was nothing negative about Lynton Viñas, but her allure made it easy for Mara to manipulate Beowulf's mind. In an instant, he had sized upon the affection Beowulf felt for Lynton, and knew that he had lustful desires which he was fighting. Boring into Beowulf's mind like a corkscrew of indulgent, lascivious, lewd depravity; he placed carnal thoughts within Beowulf's subconscious that were in oval frames of lust. He made Beowulf see her in all her alluring splendour.

Mara titillated Beowulf's libido, making him rise with lustful thoughts of Lynton in his arms, touching him, caressing him all over his body, and he touching her in satisfying pursuit of that which he had desired since the first moment when his eyes feasted upon her magnificent countenance of raw sexuality permeating every breath she took with her perfectly symmetrical breasts rising and falling in a harmonious symphony of sensuality. Her perfectly proportioned body was poetry in motion and those luscious, thick, pouty lips seemed designed to give carnal pleasure.

All this was happening in an instant of mind manipulation as Mara was adapt at reaching into the pleasure sensitive areas of the brain. He was painting a picture of carnality that floated images of an alluring Lynton across those pleasure neurons that were now firing rapidly with thoughts that Beowulf had tried to relegate to the dark corners of his mind.

Lynton Viñas and Beowulf Perez:
Demon Slayers in the Taal Inferno

Mara's eyes bored into Beowulf's eyes and Beowulf drifted into a trance of transitional desire as he began to form the ovals of lust being seared into his mind by Mara.

Lynton Viñas and Beowulf Perez:
Demon Slayers in the Taal Inferno

In Beowulf's mind, Mara planted these seeds of lust as he whispered, "Think of her lovely body and what you desire from it. Think of pressing your body against hers and wrapping her in your arms as the two of you delight in carnal blissfulness

Lynton Viñas and Beowulf Perez:
Demon Slayers in the Taal Inferno

As images formed in Beowulf's mind of the sensual Lynton, the carnal whispers of Mara dug deep into his psyche. "Think of those succulent, juicy, tasty lips that you want pressed against yours. Imagine your tongues dancing in duelling delight as waves of ecstasy sweep over you like a mighty Tsunami roaring ashore."

Lynton Viñas and Beowulf Perez:
Demon Slayers in the Taal Inferno

The whisper was haunting. "Think of those luscious breasts and how you would like to touch them."

Again, the whisper had Beowulf in a trance. "You want to feel those soft legs. You dream of what is between them and the delights it will bring. Go forth now; grab her in your arms. Embrace her as you have no other woman in your life. She is all you desire. She is life. She is the air you breathe. Without her you do not exist. Go, grab her and make her yours."

Lynton could hear nothing as Mara was using telepathy to get into Beowulf's mind and drive him wild with desire. After all, he was the demon of desire. It was he who tempted and cajoled to make desire the focus of a person's being.

Lynton tried to break the spell by shouting "Beo, Beo!" However, the intensity of Beowulf's trance-like state seemed to blot out everything but the carnal thoughts that were now running rampantly through his mind like a 100 metre runner dashing toward the finish line. He was being gradually lulled into a pleasure-filled frenzy of desire for she who stood by his side.

Suddenly, Beowulf turned to Lynton, moved quickly toward her, grabbed her violently and pulled her to him. She did not resist. She fell into his arms and whispered in his ear. "Do not let his evil capture your mind. Resist with ever fibre of your being. He wants to corrupt you, use your love for me to destroy you."

Lynton Viñas and Beowulf Perez:
Demon Slayers in the Taal Inferno

At that moment, Lynton's thoughts were of her Wayne, who would have understood her need to comfort her new friend and protect him from the manifestations of evil being invoked by Mara.

J. Wayne Frye

Lynton Viñas and Beowulf Perez:
Demon Slayers in the Taal Inferno

Mara looked down into a caldron of fire and you could see his anger. He still tried to penetrate Beowulf's inner most thoughts, but the love and compassion shown him by Lynton had broken the spell.

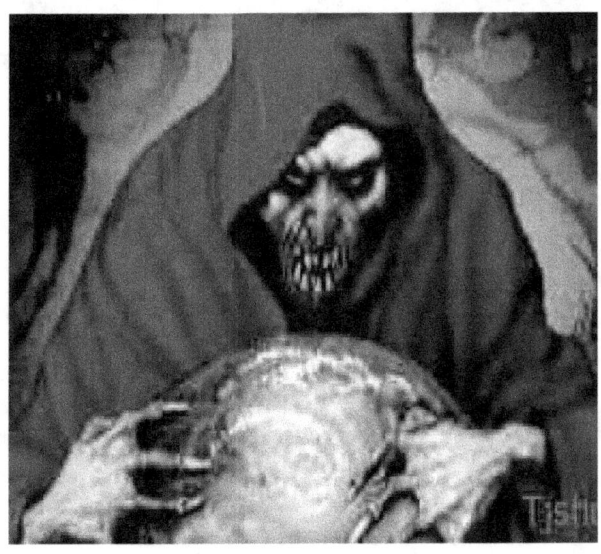

Behind Mara wrapped in a black cloak was Strududa, the skeleton of shock and awe that inhabited the minds of nation's leaders to poison them into seeking wars of conquest to wrought destruction and pestilence. He was now trying to manipulate Beo's thoughts, attempting to drive him toward self-aggrandizement through his desire for Lynton.

Lynton Viñas and Beowulf Perez:
Demon Slayers in the Taal Inferno

Lynton, letting go of Beowulf, turned and stood boldly before both demons undeterred as she said, "Lust is normal, but allowing it to control you is not. This is a good man who stands with me in my battle against evil."

Beowulf, bowing his head in shame, said to Mara, "I admit lust for her, but I shall never let it rear its ugly head again in the fight for Sarafina's soul."

Mara raised his palms upwards and said, "Lord Elashabab has greater powers than I. He, like all of us

Lynton Viñas and Beowulf Perez: Demon Slayers in the Taal Inferno

can be slain only by the just at full-moon, and neither of you is just enough to defeat his power. He will manifest himself in almost any form and devour you like a feast set on the table of tribulations which is that upon which we all feed.

Lynton, standing there in nearly naked glory had placed aside her shield and sword. She defiantly jutted out her breasts and said, "I lay down my shield and sword before you, because I have no fear of you. Give us your fire, your slime, your temptations of the flesh and we shall spit upon them as we do you and that abomination that stands behind you. Our defiance is our shield. Our sword is our devotion to justice that unlocks the door to salvation. Like Buddha before us, we shall not be tempted no matter what you lay before us. Fame, glory, money, the lure of the flesh shall not deter us from our mission."

A mighty wind suddenly came swirling down from above and the earth began to shake. Lynton began to put her breast plate back on and as she was buttoning it, a booming voice bellowed, Go and meet your fate.

Lynton Viñas and Beowulf Perez:
Demon Slayers in the Taal Inferno

J. Wayne Frye

CHAPTER 5
THE FULL-MOON ON THEIR SIDE

Confidently she strode through the corridors of fire,
Like a gazelle hopping across the plains.
Her assured, confident manner was so fine,
It was like to hell she had brought aged wine.

Lord Byron could sound her siren:
She walks in beauty, like the night
Of cloudless climes and starry skies;
And all that's best of dark and bright
Meet in her aspect and her eyes;
Thus mellowed to that tender light
Which heaven to gaudy day denies.

One shade the more, one ray the less,
Had half impaired the nameless grace
Which waves in every raven tress,
Or softly lightens o'er her face;
Where thoughts serenely sweet express,
How pure, how dear their dwelling-place.

And on that cheek, and o'er that brow,

Lynton Viñas and Beowulf Perez:
Demon Slayers in the Taal Inferno

So soft, so calm, yet eloquent,
The smiles that win, the tints that glow,
But tell of days in goodness spent,
A mind at peace with all below,
A heart whose love is innocent!

Thus all hell was in awe of her grace
She was a mighty and wondrous woman.
She was like the very finest Belgium lace,
Able and assured all power to summon
As a light from above glowed radiantly on her face
Like she was wrapped in heaven's blanket.

Episode VI

The bold in battle, either die or survive to fight another day. Lynton and Beowulf had survived their confrontation with the demon Mara giving tit-for-tat. Their inexorable fate lay before them and they did not dither in meeting it. Erect and with determined strides they progressed through the mire and muck of the hell that lay before them, in search of he who had Sarafina and was going to suck her soul out of her body.

J. Wayne Frye

Lynton Viñas and Beowulf Perez:
Demon Slayers in the Taal Inferno

Lynton, filled with admiration and respect, turned to Beowulf and with deep sincerity, said, "I have meandered these corridors of fire before, but whether it was a reality or a dream I cannot be sure. However, that time I was alone while my trusted friends, Channa and Ingrid, waited in a house where spirits longed to be released from their agony. This time I am proud and privileged to have you by my side in the place where evil dwells, friend."

Beowulf felt euphoric that Lynton would call him friend and that she would feel confident in his abilities. Moving forward, they came upon the lair of the demon Resheph, known as the demon of plagues in the Old Testament. He enjoyed raining down terror on masses. His pleasure was in seeing mass suffering from disease that he joyfully spread. His was an evil that saw pleasure in bringing misery to as many as possible at one time. No doubt, he took great pleasure in seeing George Bush practice mass terror from 80,000 feet in Iraq by using carpet bombing to incinerate innocent men, women and children in that abomination called democracy building, which was a code word for mayhem and misery for those America deemed an impediment to the march of capitalist exploitation.

Above Resheph flew Aswangs, the mythical Filipino bloodsucking creatures, and below him were souls begging for release that would never come. He ignored them but you could tell that their misery brought him great joy.

"Ah, you are the little one known as the demon fighter," Resheph laughed. "What a joke you are. You disgusting little bitch, and he who is with you is equally disgusting – nothing more than an urchin of the streets. Elashabab will have you for his lunch and regurgitate your remains into the lake of fire."

Lynton Viñas and Beowulf Perez: Demon Slayers in the Taal Inferno

Lynton, before Resheph in all her nearly naked magnificent glory, unashamed and unabashedly determined to battle Elashabab for Sarafina's soul, took a deep breath, her perfectly symmetrical breasts rising in synchronized harmony and her toned, tight, muscular derriere glistening in the reflective light from the blazing fires all about, and said, "I am little in stature, but I am not little in determination. I am not a woman you want to mess with, even if you are a demon."

Lynton stood before him in nakedness, but he scoffed at her boldness "Ha, your nakedness is disgusting. You think it gives you courage to be unashamed, but I look upon your body and want to regurgitate, because your body is as disgusting as the sun that shines to start each day. You want beauty; look around me at all these naked people who are suffering. Their misery is naked before me and all the demons that inhabit this place of eternal pain."

Lynton pointed at him, without her shield and sword, as monstrous creatures of evil swirled all about her feet. She said, without fear, "I am naked before you,

Lynton Viñas and Beowulf Perez:
Demon Slayers in the Taal Inferno

because I am not ashamed and my life is pure as are my thoughts."

Roaring with raucous laughter and indifferent disregard, Resheph caused the earth around them to shake which made Lynton and Beowulf unsteady on their feet. They grabbed one another to steady themselves. He said, "I have shared this wonderful lair with Lord Elashabab the Magnificent for thousands of years. I have watched him capture the souls of many, and not one has he ever lost. Some of the greatest demon fighters have gone into psychological and physical battles with him, and they have all lost, many losing their own soul in the process, so be prepared little lady. This is not a game you are playing."

The horror of Elashabab was revered throughout hell, and he sent a message to Lynton by way of a grotesque creature he had adopted from the souls he had made his. The poor thing was called Danemoto. Through clenched teeth he said, "My master sends you greetings."

He then let out a sinister laugh just as Resheph patted him on the back. "You are a welcome guest in his fiery home here on Luzon. To you this message my master sends: "Your kin he knows as he has devoured many of them as they lived less than virtuous lives above, hardy heroes they thought they were, but now they writhe in the hot fires here, their souls tormented for eternity. He knows you have heard of that which makes him a mortal and subject to death, but do not think you can conjure up that which would make him vulnerable to your sword which you think is righteous. You are indeed a formable foe and he looks forward to the battle, but first you must get to him. Good luck, because what lies ahead for you is a journey of hardship and despair. Your friend Beowulf is also welcome, but he will die, as will you, a horrible, excruciatingly painful death that will make all who dwell here euphoric."

Lynton said, "We all die. What counts is if we die with dignity."

Danemoto as He Appeared to Lynton and Beowulf

The dynamic dynamo had plenty to say to Danemoto. "Return to your inglorious master and tell him that my nerve is steady and my might growing each minute that passes here, and that he, on the other hand, is growing weaker, because his evil cannot stand against the might of the righteous." She then reached down for her sword which glistened in the light of the roaring fires all about. "This is my indignation that I wield with commitment to defend the defenceless."

She then reached for her shield, polished to shine like a mirror. She brandished it in such a manner that she turned it toward her and that magnificent body honed for battle and perfectly shaped with tautness seemed to permeate into the metal and burn an image of a woman of steel into it that appeared to pulsate with determination.

"Tell that monstrous entity Elashabab that I slaughter demons when the moon is full as it is on this very day, because it makes demons vulnerable to the sword that has been tempered with the blood of evil ones."

She reached down and took up her sword. A bright aura seemed to form about her, and she shined like a great beacon in the darkness.

Lynton Viñas and Beowulf Perez:
Demon Slayers in the Taal Inferno

TJS Conversion depiction of Lynton with fiery red hair and wings as she faced off with Danemoto

Brandishing the sword that was bigger than she was, she suddenly sprouted the wings of an avenging angel. She embellished the sword's history and her prowess to make a point. "Over the hills and valleys in Laguna I slew demons one night with this mighty weapon, as two kind souls were in need and faced great peril that required I crush the grim ones who were tormenting them. Elashabab now, monster cruel,

Lynton Viñas and Beowulf Perez:
Demon Slayers in the Taal Inferno

shall be mine to quell in single battle, and I have with me the mighty Beowulf who has a history of fighting demons for the church."

Eyes ablaze with fury, she continued. "We have wandered far but we have mighty shields with us to ward off the evil and we have swords honed from a metal brought from another world. It is the metal of righteousness and indignation. Ah, and the shield is a warrior's shield that is tempered too with metal that does not yield before evil. It has the might of the heavens far away from whence came a superhuman race that never cowered before demons, as they had weapons that were fortified against he who lurks in darkness to send out his minions to capture the souls of men in a world that he rules without question, because governments, the rich, the privileged are the servants of Beelzebub, who bought their souls with money."

Again, rhythmically heaving those magnificent breasts that were like small mountain peaks piercing the heavens to bring peace and tranquility, she said, "I alone, with my mighty comrade here, this hardy man of righteousness, scorn Elashabab and the evil he represents. I front the fiend and fight for life, foe against foe as I refuse to allow such strife. You see, I fear not death, for life without courage already has put the one who breathes with no courage under the sod. Living without courage is not living. If death must take me; and my blood-covered body he'll bear as prey, ruthlessly devouring it, the evil-one, with my life-blood reddening his lair shall know that he has fought one who asked no quarter and gave no quarter."

Though he was a servant of his lord, Elashabab, Danemoto was actually impressed by the dynamic dynamo. He bowed his head and snorted small green slime from his nostrils, but you could see he had been awed by the words from Lynton who feared no man, nor any demon.

Episode VII

Instinctively, Lynton and Beowulf knew the way they must trod, and they turned from the two evil ones who sit in disbelief that one so small could be so brave.

Lynton Viñas and Beowulf Perez: Demon Slayers in the Taal Inferno

Lynton looked over at Beowulf and whispered, "What a liar I am, but I fooled them didn't I?"

Smiling back Beowulf replied, "I am fooled, too."

"The *Los Angeles Times* once called my dear Wayne a marketing genius. I learned from the best. I really fooled those two with embellishments?"

"And me."

Their camaraderie had developed into mutual trust and respect. Lynton said, "Combat is as much in the mind as the body. Sore is my soul to say that with you by my side, I feel braver my dear Beowulf. Together, we hate that which evil has wrought. I know that if all others fail me, you shall always be by my side."

Beowulf's admiration for Lynton grew with each passing minute. She was the epitome of steadfastness, devotion and goodness. They had probably only been in this den of inequity for a few minutes, but it seemed like days as they slowly traversed ever forward, now almost oblivious to the fires that were consuming the poor souls who were damned to the evil place. And some places they passed there were no fires, just people agonizing in misery as they knew the fires were waiting for them and that this horrendous hell was going to last for an eternity.

Passing over a red hot bridge where people were crucified below upside down and the poor souls were begging for mercy, one could see what devastation was wrought by Elashabab. One female soul was begging with great trepidation, "Elashabab used the terror of the blades to pierce me and hang me here by the bridge, but death will not come, as I am doomed to suffer forever. I know you demon fighter. Turn back. He is too powerful to be defeated."

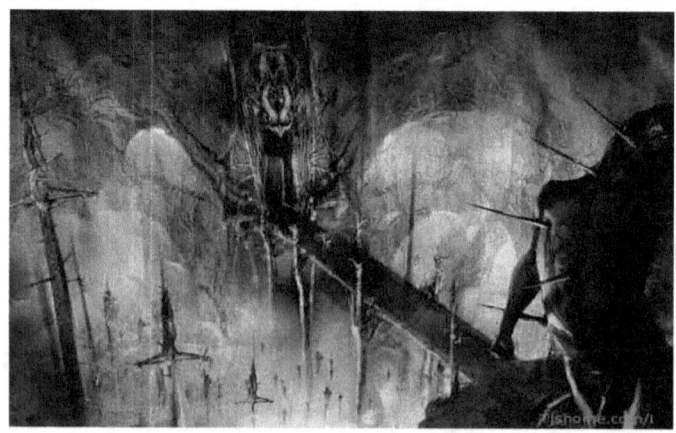

Lynton Viñas and Beowulf Perez:
Demon Slayers in the Taal Inferno

Lynton, undeterred said, "I am sorry for your suffering, despite what you may have done. If it is any consolation, I am about to slay Elashabab. It will not end your suffering, but it may ease your soul."

"Thank you demon fighter; all here know you well and we hope you can slay Elashabab."

Suddenly, as they crossed the bridge and came to a clearing a bevy of arrows came hurtling through the air and the bloodied Lynton extended her shield and warded them off as buzzards circled behind her.

Scraped and bruised by some of the arrows, Beowulf quickly rushed to her side, but she bade him not to worry with words of wisdom. "It is better to conquer yourself than to win a thousand battles. Then the victory is yours. It cannot be taken from you, not by angels or by demons, heaven or hell. We are here for ourselves as well as Sarafina, because we are conquering our own fears. Together Beowulf, we are a mighty team."

Smiling, he replied, "Yes, we are."

Episode VIII

These two were unbound from the conventional restraints of mortals. They had some how crossed over into a nether world of immortals. They were both galled by the misery they saw, and determined to see that Sarafina did not suffer the same fate as those others whose souls were in such torment.

These two were the envy of angels on high and demons down below, because they were freed from traditional restraints. They were the mighty demon hunters in the lair of Elashabab. No thing living or dead could dissuade them from their appointed mission.

So weaned they all restraint as they undertook this grand adventure as if it was a buffet of delight to battle a demon. Nearly naked with sword by her side, Lynton was a force that was like a wind that whistled through the hollows of a valley where hope reigned. She would sweep away sorrow. By her side was the lion, Beowulf, mighty and strong to be her dependable right arm.

Together, nothing could divide them. Churning waves of fire and evil demons that blocked the way, darkling malcontent, and the ruthless rushes of pleading souls could not braid their determined breasts that beat with hearts of righteousness. They grasped a firm and determined hatred for the foe, with grimmest gripe. 'Twas granted them almost as if from on-high the will to pierce the monster with point of sword, with blade of battle the huge beast of the evil one Beelzebub who had appointed Elashabab and Abbaddon as soul gathers. Their beef was with

Lynton Viñas and Beowulf Perez:
Demon Slayers in the Taal Inferno

Elashabab, but heaven help any other demon that might get in their way.

Episode IX

The evil monsters thronging together had decided to impede these two on their quest. They embraced the evil then to devour their victims' souls, vengeful creatures, seated to banquet at the bottom of hell's pit they lay in wait.

The two intrepid determined demon fighters seemed to have a light following them, almost as if it was a light of love and devotion. Was it a beacon of righteousness?

In the far distance were imposing towering mountains with winding walls red with the look of evil. Never beneath evil's dome was there a more desolate, barren, forsaken looking place. Still, traversing through this evil the two knew that the soul of a young woman was on the other side waiting to be plucked from the body and placed in eternal servitude to the evil one if they were not there to defend her.

J. Wayne Frye

Lynton Viñas and Beowulf Perez:
Demon Slayers in the Taal Inferno

Oh, this place before them reeked of unmerciful, malicious, hideous vileness.

No wiser two had ever treaded this ground of such fallacious terror and bitter misery. No two in play of war between good and evil ever performed a more daring deed. I boast not of it at all, but simply state facts as they are. These brethren so dear cursed evil that lay cold, heartless and uncompromising before them. Never had the mighty demon Elashabab two greater warriors fought. But speedily now the two moved ever forward to prove the prowess and pride that bid them do battle in the pit of fire to which Sarafina had unconsciously descended. Blithe to mead went the two that listened to the beat of a different drummer and with them went the light of dawn that would shine on a brighter tomorrow morning over the inhabitants of that little village at the base of the mighty Taal.

Suddenly, Lynton turned to Beowulf and said, "Give me your trusty sword and take my shield. The succubus is to our right and she will try to lure you into her arms so she can suck out your soul. Do not look upon her; use both shields to deflect her glare of rancorous evil. With two mighty swords, I shall slay the tempter snake that wraps its depraved villainy about her.

Beowulf did not question. He handed her his sword and kneeled down, placing the two shields in front of him for protection from the succubus.

Lynton Viñas and Beowulf Perez:
Demon Slayers in the Taal Inferno

Lynton's Swords of Righteousness by Freddie Perez

With two swords in her strong hands, she turned to her right and looked upon evil as her swords glistened, reflecting the light of righteousness. Blood was still on her body, but it was the blood from her encounter with the arrows, so it was her purified blood that was ready to be spilled again for her friend. There, evil permeating from her, was the succubus who was wrapped in rapture with the snake of temptation.

She embraces the darkness,
the siren-demon who will creep
into shadowed chambers of the mind
to seductively invade sin's sleep.
Her raven locks cascading,
her skin pale white, pristine,
her lips so warm, persuading
men to seep into the dream,
submit to her evil passions,
allow her to sap their strength.
Passion slowly arising, knowing
men go to absolutely any length
to embrace her cunning warmth,
willingly sinking to any depth
allowing permission to rob the soul
of all power, even of life's breath.
Each second makes a man weaker.
It becomes harder to resist.
Soon she will suck him in
as her lips seem to beg for a kiss.
Her mission then accomplished,

J. Wayne Frye

Lynton Viñas and Beowulf Perez:
Demon Slayers in the Taal Inferno

her job done so very well,

she'll just move on to another,

seeking soul after soul to fell,

to capture and make each one

reside with her in hell.

**The Succubus of the Taal Inferno
Photographic Reproduction
by Freddie Perez**

Lynton Viñas and Beowulf Perez: Demon Slayers in the Taal Inferno

Looking down at Lynton, the succubus even tried to seduce her. "Do you not desire me little one? Am I not alluring to you. Look at my luscious body that is made for pleasure, then turn and tell your friend behind you to take down his shields, for I am not to be feared. I am to be loved, loved in all its glory where inhibitions float onto the sweet breeze of carnal pleasure. Come naked one, you obviously have no inhibitions. Come and we three may share pleasure as is only dreamed by most."

I truly do not understand the reason why,
Mortals run from me as if they would die.
I am a gentle soul that may be a little quirky,
But that should not make anyone so weary.
I will admit that I may appear a little scary,
My snake lover makes me red and fiery.
Still that is no excuse to run from this lady,
After all do I not strike you as being sexy?

It is true that I like things on the side of gory,
And that I do enjoy things being a little bloody.
Fire and pain are elements I enjoy so dearly,
And I use them both well never feeling sorry.

Lynton Viñas and Beowulf Perez:
Demon Slayers in the Taal Inferno

Join me in ecstasy as this you should not miss,
For death is only the start of my little story.
You see, death with me is actually glory
For we shall fornicate together in bliss.

Come now little one, drop your swords
And have him behind you lose his shields.
Embrace me and my snake lover,
And we shall frolic in pleasure's fields.
You want this thrill I can sense.
Go ahead and drop that rough exterior
And stop all this righteous pretence.
Satan's love is always superior!

Lynton had known lust as have all and she considered it a natural part of life, but when it became the lure of evil intentions, it was an abomination. She looked into the succubus's eyes and recited her own poem:

Seduction wicked succubus
Spoken words and twisted deeds
Come from your siren call
Play with lustful thoughts

Lynton Viñas and Beowulf Perez:
Demon Slayers in the Taal Inferno

Be a wicked toy

Feel the caress of silken words

Hear the words

Watch her dance

Spoken poison

Twisted mind

Seductive sex goddess

Toy with the minds

Selfish little boys

Sunken by beauty

It is not your body

She wants in harmony

It is your soul

Caressing the snake in ecstasy laden delight, the succubus said, "Temptation is my stock and trade. You are a wily one, and your body makes me jealous, but also stirs my lust. What say we two leave that one hiding behind the shield and retire to my den of lust?"

Jutting her chest out, making her perky breasts rise and fall in perfect synchronization, Lynton said, "You bleed in the shadows of woe. I feel nothing as your eyes gaze upon me. Haunted with abominable lust

Lynton Viñas and Beowulf Perez:
Demon Slayers in the Taal Inferno

you linger with a necrotic glow. I feel nothing but pity for your hardened soul. Hush with your temptations; it is time to be silent as my duty calls. Go fourth to the abyss below that summons your wantonness and wander the coils of fathomless misery to which you are doomed and want to doom others. Be gone with you or I shall use my righteous swords to slay that evil snake which you embrace, leaving you to ponder in loneliness why you must forever seek to degrade others as you have degraded yourself. I feel pity for you, as in life you must have born great misery in your lust that replaced love."

The succubus, defeated with words rather than swords, bowed her head and said, "You are brave little one. You will need all that bravery in your battle against Elashabab." There was sincerity in her voice as she said, "You are right, in life I allowed lust to guide me and I paid the price by never really finding love. I am Lilith."

"I know you Lilith. You were Adam's first wife in the Garden of Eden. You mated with the archangel Samuel and refused to return to Adam as your lust overruled your heart. You, along with Mahalath, Agrat, Bat Mahlat and Naamah were the five original succubi."

"Little one, you know your theological history very well. I commend and salute you on your superior knowledge of that which most people are totally ignorant. Ignorance is what gives us much of our power, and the world is filled with those who are content to let others do their thinking for them. You will need that knowledge as you make your way to he who spits fire."

Lynton nodded and said, as she lowered her swords, "Lilith, I bid you adieu and say, without any reservation, that you are indeed a woman of incredible beauty who could tempt any man, mortal or immortal. I cannot wish you well, but I do wish you peace."

Episode X

Beowulf handed Lynton her shield, took his sword back and the two began the rest of their journey. They walked past an area on their left with people pleading and begging for an end to their agony.

As they progressed toward those mountains that loomed in the distance, off to their right a voice called, "Ah, the demon fighters are here. I am Alonosobar, and I guard the cave that goes into the valley on the other side of the mountain. I shall not let you go there before my master Elashabab has taken the young girl's soul. Stop you two or suffer dire consequences."

Lynton turned, dropped her sword, shield and removed the last of the garments that covered her. On her left Beowulf stood dumbfounded, but she winked at him and whispered, "He is only vulnerable on his left side where he was once pierced by the same Roman soldier who pierced the flesh of Jesus. He was healed by Jesus, but he still rejected him for the love of Lilith whom we have met. You know what to do my friend while I distract him.

She moved naked toward the demon that was flapping its wings. "I know you demon. You are the demon of love that lures women to your arms so that they can melt with pleasure in your embrace. Come, I cannot resist that embrace that brings untold joy. Pull me close to you, so that our bodies can meld as one and we can float in blissfulness in this place of eternal fire. I no longer care about that girl. Let her soul rot here and see how much I care."

Lynton Viñas and Beowulf Perez: Demon Slayers in the Taal Inferno

Smiling, Alonosobar said, "You do not fool me woman. You are up to something, but it matters not. If you have the courage to embrace me, then I shall own your soul. Come forward if you dare and feel my embrace that will melt your heart and fill it with desire for that which I offer.

"I come with bated breath for your embrace."

Freddie Perez Depiction of Lynton In Alonosobar's Embrace

Beowulf very slyly made his way to Alonosobar's left side, and as he was embracing Lynton, Beowulf, without hesitation, simply slid the sword into the demon's side.

Elashabab raised his head and moaned, letting loose of Lynton who stepped back in her naked glory and said, "You were healed by a just man and turned your back on him. Like him, your side was been pierced, and I say to you, fall upon the ground and we shall walk over you into the valley of the shadow of death and face Elashabab. I am Lynton Viñas and this is my friend Beowulf Perez. We are here to slay Elashabab, because it is written that demons are vulnerable at full-moon. You Alonosobar are going to die now, for you have been pierced by the sword of retribution at full-moon.

He fell to the ground and stared up, saying, "Oh no."

Lynton, smiling down at him said, "Die demon, die!" She stepped over him, looked down and said, "I wish I had my high heels from hell to pierce your evil and grind you under my heel into oblivion. This is your final day of evil, demon of darkness. You have come up against Lynton and Beowulf – demon slayers."

Lynton Viñas and Beowulf Perez:
Demon Slayers in the Taal Inferno

Episode X1

The two walked to the fiery cave entrance and stood there determined and unafraid. Like Wyatt Earp and Doc Holiday ready to walk into the O.K Corral and face the Clanton's in history's greatest shootout, they were prepared to walk into the pit of evil and face the fierce demon that had violated the sanctity of a young woman. This was their high noon.

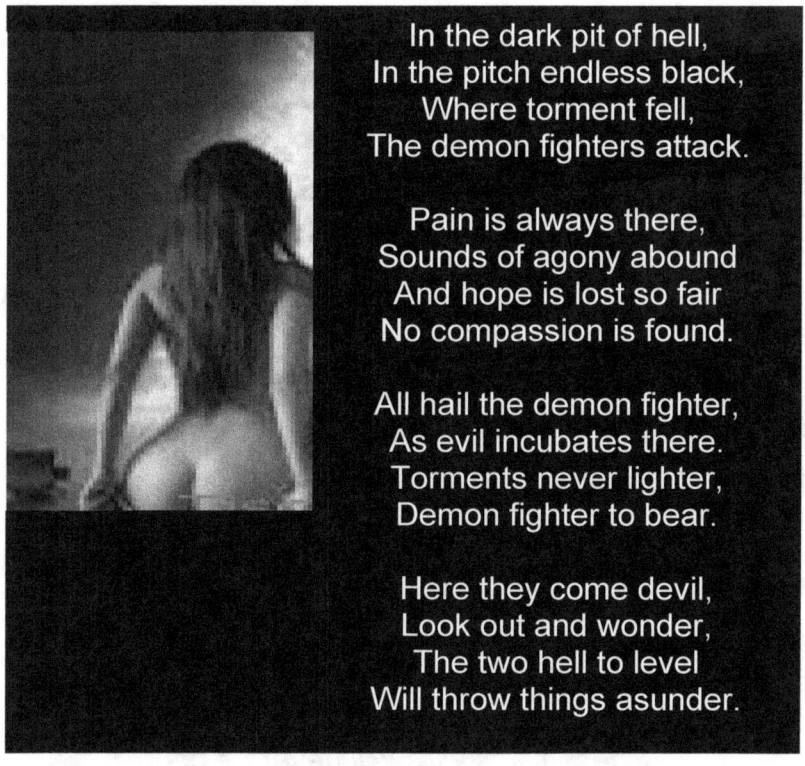

In the dark pit of hell,
In the pitch endless black,
Where torment fell,
The demon fighters attack.

Pain is always there,
Sounds of agony abound
And hope is lost so fair
No compassion is found.

All hail the demon fighter,
As evil incubates there.
Torments never lighter,
Demon fighter to bear.

Here they come devil,
Look out and wonder,
The two hell to level
Will throw things asunder.

Lynton Viñas and Beowulf Perez: Demon Slayers in the Taal Inferno

INTO THE RING OF FIRE

They knew they must continue pursuit.

Bowed they before no demon.

They were not a flee'in.

Through the cave of fire they went,

Energy of theirs nearly spent.

This was the road chosen by they,

Legends of their bravery would say.

These two faced hell undeterred.

Their mission could not be deferred.

Into the valley of the shadow of death,

Moving ever forward with bated breath.

Elashabab had Sarafina spread upon his plate,

As the two demon fighters feared her fate.

They shall not be deterred from their call,

Even if in death they might finally fall.

All around them were tormented mournful cries,

Where all hope unceremoniously dies.

Those souls to the devil were already lost,

But Sarafina should not have to pay the cost.

Chards of fire rain down from above.

Still, they never quit when push comes to shove.

Light the fires of hell with ill intent.

These two's wills will never be bent.

J. Wayne Frye

Lynton Viñas and Beowulf Perez:
Demon Slayers in the Taal Inferno

Lynton stood at the entrance to the cave and suddenly an image of the devil appeared. A booming, deep voice said, "Enter at your own risk."

Lynton Viñas and Beowulf Perez:
Demon Slayers in the Taal Inferno

The two ignored the warning and walked into the cave that would lead to the valley where they would be in the shadow of death. They walked out the other side and Lynton put her shield down and stood staring at a light in the distance that reminded her of a full-moon and the fact that Elashabab was vulnerable now. She picked up her weapons as did Beo and they had no fear, because they had their swords, shields and the full-moon on their side.

J. Wayne Frye

CHAPTER 6
OUT INTO THE SUNSHINE OF HOPE
WHERE PEACE AND TRANQUILITY REIGNED

Two Who Refused to be Broken

Just like a Wild West posse that rode into town
Weaving a whirlwind of chaos up and down.
Beo and Lynton had the demon on the run.
He hoped they would come undone.

All becomes quiet when determined eyes meet,
Watching as the demon fighters would not retreat.
They would never pay the demon's fee
Determined to let what was coming be.

Their eyes are narrowed as they stare.
Their intentions were easy to declare.
They had left no room for debate
To face Elashabab who was filled with hate.

They stood mighty the two together,
Comrades in bad or fair weather.
They were ready to battle against the dark.

Lynton Viñas and Beowulf Perez: Demon Slayers in the Taal Inferno

They had received heaven's spark.

The truth was a sword piercing evil's heart.
These two demon fighters would never part.
In a maelstrom of despotic evil oft spoken,
These two refused to ever be broken.

Episode XII

Onward led the barren road again through the sad uncoloured plain of hopelessness that was reflected in the starkness of despair that permeated all about. Under light brooding and dim and along the utmost rim of the towering mountains they traversed tepidly and with caution. Wall and rampart risen to sight cast a shadow not of night, but of an evil darkness that was blacker than night. Beyond them seemed to glow bonfires lit with human souls as cries of agony reverberated throughout the valley. Tired from their incessant onward march, at a stream that was not hot with fire they fell to splash water on their faces.

Beowulf looked to his right at Lynton and said, "I am worn and weary, but with you by my side I have am elated and filled with the energy of utter righteousness.

Lynton Viñas and Beowulf Perez:
Demon Slayers in the Taal Inferno

I am your comrade dear Lynton, and I shall not hesitate to die by your side, if such action becomes necessary."

Weary, but undeterred, Beowulf rose and smiled at Lynton. "Let's go demon fighter, we have demon butt to kick."

Lynton Viñas and Beowulf Perez: Demon Slayers in the Taal Inferno

And they knew they must continue pursuit.
Bowed they before no demon,
They were not a flee'in.
Through the cave of fire they went,
Energy of theirs nearly spent.
This was the road chosen by they;
Legends of their bravery would say.
These two faced hell undeterred;
Their mission could not be deferred.

For a long time they walked along a corridor of fire with no words spoken. And in the darkness Beowulf broke the silence when he pointed ahead to his right, saying, "I think it not conjecture to say that there in the distance is an altar with someone lying on it before a demon-like creature."

Lynton sighed, "We are here my friend. Get ready for battle. I want you to know that it has been a pleasure having you by my side. I am sorry that I could not return your romantic love Beowulf, as you are a good and decent man." Then she laughed as she said, "When we get back I have a friend I want you to meet."

162   J. Wayne Frye

Lynton Viñas and Beowulf Perez: Demon Slayers in the Taal Inferno

"I'll take you up on it. I hope she is rich as well a pretty."

Moving ever forward, she replied, "Pretty yes, rich, however, is a rarity in the Philippines."

Hard as yet the eye could see the eternal masonry of manic evil in the distance. To the left of the altar, there in the dark to and fro there stirred a spark as the now sombre two gripped their swords with fervour. Dully at the blackened sky staring, and with idle eye measuring the listless plain, Lynton said, "He senses we are near, but he turns not for he wants to show indifference."

They began to think again. Many things they thought of then. The coming battle, of course, but Beowulf reflected on his life of abject poverty and desertion by his mother, and how he was now the richest man alive because he had Lynton by his side. On the other hand, dear Lynton reflected on her Wayne, whom she had rescued from the doldrums of despair, which had fostered love and affection that had grown and prospered over time

Lynton Viñas and Beowulf Perez:
Demon Slayers in the Taal Inferno

Lynton looked over at Beo and knew he was thinking of her. She smiled and said, "Stop it. Think of the women you have loved physically and emotionally. Think of the cities entered, oceans crossed, knowledge gained and virtue lost." She could not help but laugh at the last one, because men always reflected nostalgically on the sexual peccadilloes which seemed to be so important to them. She continued. "Think of cureless folly done and said, and the lovely friendship that led us to this pit of everlasting fire."

Against a smoulder dun and a dawn now without a sun did the nearing bastion loom where evil was dancing with Sarafina. And across the gate of gloom they moved slowly forward when a furious winged demon blocked their way. Breathing fire from its nostrils it had no speech, but with her mighty sword Lynton lunged at its chest and pierced it causing a painful cry. It reached down to grab her, but as it did, Beowulf plunged his sword into its right side and it belched fire that scorched his forehead. In and out, in and out, they both furiously plunged until green slime poured out onto the ground and the demon collapsed.

Lynton Viñas and Beowulf Perez:
Demon Slayers in the Taal Inferno

Suddenly, they quickened the pace, mindful of time and place. Other demons awaited, but they did not tarry as time was growing short, the full moon to be gone soon. There was another sentry like before. Ever darker hell on high reared its strength upon the crimson sky. Slinging swords from side to side and using their shields as a battering ram they forged ahead pushing demons aside. They stayed right on the track, fletching the daunting echo of righteousness by their side. But in the distance Elashabab was pacing now, looking down at Sarafina knowing her soul had to be stolen soon or the time would elapse.

Lynton Viñas and Beowulf Perez:
Demon Slayers in the Taal Inferno

Elashabab, nursing his tormented pride, turned his head to neither side but looked down upon his victim and began to wave his hands over her head. He sunk deep into his task calling upon the hell-fire in his heart.

They were almost there now, but against their entering into the altar area from the side of a mountain filled with death and sin raised a demon to render key and sword to his devil lord. And the other demons all about foul to see lifted up their eyes with no plea. Then they all turned their heads, looked, and knew evil would be fed once these two were dead. Not stirred, Lynton naked and proud stood her ground, but misinterpreted where Beo was as he had engaged another demon in battle, and she fell into the demon's clutches. To a nearby pole he lashed her hands behind her tightly and laughed as she squirmed in an attempt to free herself.

In a flash, Beo was there, slew the demon with one mighty swing of his sword and immediately freed Lynton from her bonds and together they moved toward the altar.

Lynton Viñas and Beowulf Perez:
Demon Slayers in the Taal Inferno

Freddie Perez Caricature of a Bound Lynton

Elashabab turned from the altar and waved his hands, commanding other demons to stop their progress forward. He stood up straight as he now appeared as a fiery figure ready to rain terror upon these two who dared enter his lair to free Sarafina from his spell.

Lynton Viñas and Beowulf Perez:
Demon Slayers in the Taal Inferno

He was seething with intense anger now with fire swirling round him as he commanded not with voice but a primal force of will that made the demons react with ferocity toward Lynton and Beowulf, their swords raining terror upon the demons who had never been challenged before with such verve, grit and determination.

Lynton Viñas and Beowulf Perez:
Demon Slayers in the Taal Inferno

They fell one by one and Lynton signalled Beo to ward off the remaining two demons as she made her way to Elashabab. She could only make out his silhouette in the darkness to her left, but Beo was in a ferocious battle with two winged demons that had him by the arms as he had dropped his sword and shield. She wanted to rush to his side, but he hollered, "Save Sarafina, please."

They were trying to rip his arms off, but his strength was greater than theirs. The two demons both fell into a heap, exhausted from the fierce battle.

Lynton Viñas and Beowulf Perez:
Demon Slayers in the Taal Inferno

Caught by surprise at the ferocity of the two, Elashabab turned his back on Sarafina who lay on the altar in a trance to confront Lynton. Finally, he spoke in a voice so loud that it reverberated throughout his lair, ringing ears of demon and human alike. "I shall eat your entrails bitch whore."

Lynton, without any fear in her voice, replied, "You forget it is the full moon. This Elashabab is the end of your thousands of years reigning in your evil empire. There will be no 48th victim and no catastrophic release of terror from the 16 volcanoes. This is the day you die."

In a fury, he charged toward her with fire surrounding him sending all about a seething hum. As a queen of demon slayers who comes leading conquest of evil from afar, wielding sword as she used her shield to ward off the fire he breathed she suddenly penetrated his fiery shield, plunging in and out, in and out. And the thrill of triumph waited as Lynton opened wide hell's impenetrable gates to move to the altar where Sarafina lay, now slowly awakening.

J. Wayne Frye

Lynton Viñas and Beowulf Perez: Demon Slayers in the Taal Inferno

Across the entry straddled the revolting Elashabab, whom she had wounded with arsenals brandished with righteousness in this hell. Mortally wounded, he still tried to summon his evil spell. And beside him, exhausted from battle, Beowulf crawled, reached upwards and plunged his sword into his side, eliciting a howling roar of surprise that his reign of terror was about to end.

Sin to left and death to right, Lynton quickly moved to the altar. Tuned with loving countenance, she unbound the awakened Sarafina. Their embrace was long and intense and Lynton, pointing over to the exhausted Beowulf still lying on the ground, said, "He is a mighty warrior of righteousness who slew many more demons than I. Be aware that you are free of that demon now. "

Beo raised his hand slightly, but his exhaustion was over-powering him. As Lynton walked over, with Sarafina by her side, they helped him to his feet to begin the journey back. They all looked down at the great Elashabab that was a hulk of seething flesh, green slime pouring out from his mortal wounds.

Lynton Viñas and Beowulf Perez:
Demon Slayers in the Taal Inferno

Suddenly, he arose in a flash of hate and reached out as if to beg for mercy from those who had defeated him. A raging inferno of liquid fire swept up from the ground and engulfed him. He, who had inflicted so much pain, was now afflicted with pain. He received no sympathy from the three, who turned their backs and walked away.

J. Wayne Frye

Lynton Viñas and Beowulf Perez:
Demon Slayers in the Taal Inferno

Of the roaring flaming misery that was all around them, over the deep darkness that surrounded them, the three were free. There was no anger left within them now, only relief as in the distance lightning bristled followed by thunder. It was as if hell itself was bowing in supplication to the mighty Beowulf and Lynton.

They moved steadily back toward the cave entrance, leaving behind the intense hollowness of a hell where its evil master fell. The flickering lightning was still making its definitive stroke, but the two mighty demon fighters already spoke with sword in hand that they now tossed aside since the foe had been dispatched.

Tyranny and terror flown now left a grand pair of friends alone. And beneath the nether crimson of hell's sky, the two demon fighters could only sigh. Silent, nothing found to say, they began the backward way; and the ebbing lustre died as they stood by each other's side, leaving behind the eternal fire. In silence they looked back, but behind them everything was mute, for a little bit of hell had died that day when two

Lynton Viñas and Beowulf Perez:
Demon Slayers in the Taal Inferno

brave warriors descended into the raging fires to rescue she who had fallen victim to evil. They walked the road of promise through the cave, up through the caldera and out into the sunshine of hope where peace and tranquility reigned.

Lynton Viñas and Beowulf Perez: Demon Slayers in the Taal Inferno

EPILOGUE
HIS LIFE SLOWLY EBBED AWAY

While the red-stains melt away,
of the battle won there is a ring
across the infinite expanse of day.
These two's glory can be seen
as goodness begins its reign.
The memories of this day will melt away;
as a monstrous frenzy ran its course
that led to demons which could not hold sway.
They underestimated the demon fighter,
on nature's breast, who stood against evil,
and made people's hearts lighter.
The gleam of hope, the incense-laden air,
make the demon fighters lie in sweet repose.
The warrior is in a cloud of murmured prayer,
and only wakes when weeping mothers bow
with tells of Lynton and Beowulf in Elashabab's lair.
Oh, they now forget that which was foul.
Themselves in euphoria, wrapped in old black shawls
off to church to give thanks for deliverance,
and their last small coin into the coffer falls,
while heroes are received with indifference.

J. Wayne Frye   175

Lynton Viñas and Beowulf Perez:
Demon Slayers in the Taal Inferno

Episode XIII

Bold, but without arrogance, mysterious, but not dark, Lynton Viñas was a mighty woman who had gone into hell with her friend and won the battle for a soul. She was the kind of girl, who with a half way glance, could steal your heart, mind and soul but not destroy them. Rather, she would nurture you; make you stronger, more confident and compassionate by example. She would tell you what she's thinking; she would tell you where to start and she would take your life and turn it into art. She would never leave you lonely, but she would always be free of any constraints. She was the kind of girl who could teach you the true meaning of love in a world where it was in short supply. There are times when each of us possesses that fined-tuned knowledge that we have faced adversity, hopelessness, misery and evil only to come out triumphant with a swagger of confidence that permeates our very souls. Lynton felt that way as she traversed ever upward with her two friends as the sun gradually came up over the horizon and nearly blinded all three with its intense brightness. In fact, they had to close their eyes to avoid the intensity of the light and in doing so; they briefly returned to the darkness, squinted their eyes rapidly and were suddenly in Sarafina's bedroom with her lying backwards on the bed, exhausted from her ordeal.

Lynton Viñas and Beowulf Perez:
Demon Slayers in the Taal Inferno

Beowulf lay on the floor beside the bed, obviously in deep sleep, exhausted from his ordeal. Yet, Lynton looked at the now untied Sarafina and began to wonder. Was it all a dream? Had Sarafina's superior but warped mind transported them all into the liar of a non-existent demon? Never mind, because what really mattered was that, even if it was only in her mind, the demon had been defeated.

Sarafina slowly opened her eyes and said, "Our journey of horror is over isn't it?"

"It is my sweet Sarafina, yes."

Sarafina looked over at Beo who had not stirred and said, "He is exhausted from the battle to save my soul."

"Yes, he was a mighty warrior without whom I could never have made it to the altar where Elashabab was about to suck your soul from your body and trap you in his evil liar for eternity. You owe your resurrection from the depth of depravity to a mighty warrior in the battle between good and evil."

Lynton Viñas and Beowulf Perez:
Demon Slayers in the Taal Inferno

Sarafina slowly arose from her bed and said, "I must go to church and make an offering to thank God for my deliverance."

Lynton, not seeing anything the church had actually done other than ask her and Beowulf to help, did not want to question Sarafina's fealty and devotion, so she simply did not reply. After all, the church was all most poor people had. It promised them what they were denied in this life in the afterlife.

Lynton reached down and took Sarafina's hand, leading her toward the door as they both looked back at Beowulf who still lay quietly beside the bed in blissful slumber. Sarafina's parents wrapped their arms around her, holding her so tight that one might think they would never let go. Father Vasquez nodded his head at Lynton almost with a look of disdain on his face. She eased onto the sofa and let out a sigh as Sarafina and her parents continued their embrace, sobbing tears of joy.

Lynton seemed to drift off to sleep from exhaustion, as Father Vasquez moved toward the entrance to the bedroom. He peeped back at Lynton to be sure she was asleep. Stealthily, he moved into the bedroom as he took out his handkerchief while approaching the bed. He checked to see that Beowulf was still sleeping as he dropped to his knees, looked under the bed at the pentagram there that he had, unbeknownst to Sarafina, drawn in chalk four months ago under her bed. He rubbed away the evidence of his occult practice, got up and walked to the door vowing subconsciously that he would find another victim. He stood at the door looking back at Beowulf, turned and left without noticing the blood slowly piling up on the floor beside Beowulf, who had unbeknownst to Lynton and Sarafina, suffered a mortal wound to his side in the battle. So for him, whether an adventure in reality or of the mind, he had received a critical wound and his life slowly ebbed away.

THE END

Don't Miss These Lynton Adventures
Lynton Curls Her Hair
Lynton Buys a New Cell-Phone
And Hears the Voice of Doom
Lynton Walks on Water
Lynton and the Vampire at Taygaytay Manor